The Real Story
Behind the Hurt
and The Rise
and Fall of Extremist

The Real Story Behind the Hurt and The Rise and Fall of Extremist

Josh Scott

Library of Congress Control Number:		2021909608
ISBN:	Hardcover	978-1-6641-7406-1
	Softcover	978-1-6641-7407-8
	eBook	978-1-6641-7419-1

Print information available on the last page.

Rev. date: 05/12/2021

To order additional copies of this book, contact:
Xlibris
844-714-8691
www.Xlibris.com
Orders@Xlibris.com
827175

CHAPTER 1

Approximately twenty-five years after Big Bob closed up the Hurt rock-and-roll club, he decided to visit the old club to look around. During the past twenty-five years, Big Bob was not big anymore; he had lost weight, and he looked good. He walked into the now strip club, and the inside looked about the same as when he had it. Except this time, on the stage were stripper poles and fancy lighting. Bob met up with the owner and told him he was a past owner of the club many years earlier. The club owner told Bob that the club had been doing poorly and might go up for sale.

Bob's ears perked up, and he said, "I may be interested in buying it if the price is right." They exchanged information, and a few months later, Bob got a call from the strip club owner telling him that the club was up for sale and that the asking price is negotiable.

Bob got with his attorney and came to an agreement on the price and purchased the club. A week later, the deal was done, and now it was time to make the needed changes inside and out. Bob did not like anyone losing a job, so he asked some of the girls if they wanted to stay on as waitresses; only a couple said they would, since strippers would make a lot more money stripping. Some of the bartenders also stayed on. Now a work crew came in and removed the stripper poles and some of the lighting. The signage outside was removed and changed back to The Hurt.

Bob was sentimental, and he would like to see where the old crew was and see if they were interested in coming back although they were older now. Luckily, he had some of the phone numbers, but he knew after all these years, it would be hard to find many. First on his list was Josh, but he did not have the phone number, so he called the sheriff's office to ascertain a number for Josh. Bob was told that Josh had retired a few years earlier and only had a family member's number. So Bob called it and was devastated by what he was told. The family member told Bob that just after Josh retired, he was in a terrible car crash and did not survive his injuries. Bob did not know what to say, a total wreck. Bob told the family member how sorry he was to hear this and that he did not know.

Bob asked where Josh was buried and was told he was buried in the City of Hollywood. Bob said thank you for the information and hung up. Bob was so upset that he did not make any more calls this day. Bob went home and thought back on working with Josh and how he was a great deputy sheriff. What a loss. But it was time to start hiring to fill the many positions needed. Bob also had to get the advertising going for the new rock club as well as booking the talent. After ads were placed in the paper and on Craigslist, Bob got many beautiful young girls applying for several positions. There were also numerous young men applying for bartender and barbacks. But Bob had more of an interest in hiring bouncers.

But times had changed over the years and you had to be careful how you tossed people out or you could be sued. Back in the day, when Bob was Big Bob, all the bouncers were martial artists, even his dear friend Laura, who was also a martial artist. He would have loved to have her back, but she died many years earlier from cancer and Bob had really liked her. Numerous big guys came in and applied for the bouncer positions. Bob wanted to hire at least fifteen, and those hired had to clear an extensive background check and drug screen. Eventually, Bob hired his fifteen bouncers who cleared the background and drug checks. No weapons were allowed in the club, and no employee was allowed to carry one, only a large flashlight because it was dark in the club.

Bob then started to interview some rock bands for appearances, some hard rock, some metal bands. Bob then reached out to several band members from the past, which included Johnny Depp as he was in a band called The Kids. Some of those band members were still around and lived locally. Bob called them and asked if they still had the band and if they were still in contact with Johnny Depp. Those band members advised that they were still together but had not heard from Johnny in a while. Bob asked if they could contact Johnny for a reunion play date at the opening of the club, and he was told they would try to get with him.

Bob was a reminiscent guy, and in his office, he had a plaque made up of those past employees who were no longer with us. The plaque listed Sam who was gunned down in a drive-by shooting, Richie who committed suicide in California, Laura who died from cancer, Randy who died from unknown causes, Jeff who had a heart attack, and Josh who was killed in a car crash after twenty-five years with the sheriff's office. Hopefully there would be no more names added for a while. It was now approximately one month until the opening, and things inside were coming along well. The new design was nice with new lighting and sound. The old sound-and-lighting booth was upgraded to the state of the art; it was very cool. Bob also hired a sound-and-lighting guy for the club. Now a few weeks before opening, Bob heard from one of the past members of the Kids that Johnny Depp would come out and play for the night but then had to get back to LA.

This news made Bob very happy and it meant a packed house, but he knew that he would have to have extra security due to Johnny Depp making an appearance, so he contacted the sheriff's office for six deputies to work off-duty at the club. Normally the local police would work it, but because of his friend Josh being a retired deputy and no longer with us, in his name, he wanted the sheriff's office for security. Bob also made a secure area for Depp when he came, so he would not be mobbed by fans or nonfans. It was now one week before opening, and it seemed all was well and ready to go. Bob also contacted the media for coverage, and when they heard that Depp would be there, they would be there.

Bob had obtained shirts with the club logo on them for the employees to wear. It was mandatory for all to wear them, no excuses; if you came in without it, you went home to get it. It was now opening night and the club was packed. Those working the front door had metal detectors, as each person entering was wonded and patted down to make sure no weapons were coming in and no one was sneaking in outside drinks. Tickets were sold on Ticketmaster, nowhere else. The club was a little crowded, so the local fire marshal came in and said the club was over capacity. Bob told the fire marshal, "Johnny Depp will be here tonight, and that's why we are so packed."

Johnny Depp's bus pulled up to the back of the club. He got out with some family and his bodyguard, walked over to talk with the deputies and thank them for being there. He asked about Josh, whom he knew from years earlier. Johnny was told that after he retired, he was killed in a car crash. Johnny said, "Oh shit, thanks for telling me." It was now time to start the first group, and Bob took the mic and thanked everyone for coming out to the new and improved Hurt. "And now let me introduce a band from years ago that was our house band for many years, and a very special guest: The Kids, joined by Johnny Depp." The crowd went wild holding up their cell phones taking pictures. The band played for about a half hour and exited the stage.

Johnny went backstage and met with the deputies again before getting back on his bus. Bob met with Johnny and thanked him for coming from LA and told him, "Be safe, and thanks again." Johnny got on the bus with his group and departed. Then several other bands played and rocked the house. At the end of the night, deputies helped clear the parking lot without incident. Bob was extremely happy with how things went and gathered his staff and thanked them for a job well done and then bought them all a beer. The following weeks stayed busy, and the bands that were playing were pretty good. Two of them became the house bands who played nightly.

One Saturday night, there was a domestic disturbance between a man and woman over some jealousy issue. The argument started at the table and escalated to some pushing. The bouncers intervened and told the couple to leave. The couple exited through the front door, and when outside, they started to physically fight. A bouncer at the front door stepped in to stop it when the woman pulled a small knife and stabbed the bouncer in the neck instead of her male friend. Other bouncers saw this and jumped in and tackled the woman. The bouncer that was stabbed was tended to quickly by others and quickly taken to the emergency room for treatment. The bouncer had to be taken to surgery but unfortunately succumbed to the injury because of blood loss and the cut to the jugular. The police were called, and the woman was arrested on a homicide charge.

Bob was unaware of this as he was in his office at the time. Right after the incident, he was contacted and told about the incident. He asked how his employee was and was told that his employee did not survive the stab wound. Bob fell back against the wall with tears in his eyes. Bob decided to get everyone out and close early. He wanted to know how someone came in with a knife when people were to be searched by the front door personnel. Bob then had to contact the bouncer's family and explain what had happened. Bob was beginning to think this club was cursed. Bob contacted the bouncer's family by phone and spoke to the mother. After he told her what happened, she started to cry and said, "I told him not to take that job."

Bob told her what hospital he was at so the family could get there. Bob told the mother that he would cover the funeral cost if she permitted. She did not reply then hung up. Now Bob had to put another name on his plaque. Approximately a week later, the funeral was held, and most of the club's staff was in attendance. Bob did pick up the tab for the funeral after all. Bob put stricter security measures in place for the front-door personnel. If any patron did not like the new rules, they didn't come in, and any employee skirting the rule would be fired. Bob had to hire new bouncers because some decided to leave after the stabbing. Several new guys came in for an interview, and after the background checks and drug test, they were hired.

When the two new guys started, they spoke with Bob and they asked if he was here when the bouncer was killed in the drive-by shooting years ago. Bob said yes, that he was there and that he testified against the two killers involved. The new guys said, "Wow, that's great, and did you ever think they were innocent?" Bob said no, they did it. The two new bouncers appeared to not like that answer and gave Bob a dirty look behind his back. They then went to work.

Bob got with his floor manager named Russ to work out special event nights during the year. Bob recalled that when he worked in the club on Halloween, no guns were allowed as part of a costume and told Russ to put that information on the flyer when it was time. Russ agreed as he did not want any problems. Russ was in charge of putting the advertising flyers together and mailing them out. Bob and Russ made two nights a week ladies' night; ladies had no cover and got one drink. One night a week was first responders' night. Anyone that was a first responder had no cover and got a free drink as long as they had their government ID. Certain holidays also got special attention, and one weekend day a month, there was no cover for anyone, and the cover was $15 normally. With all the upgrades Bob did to the club, he had no problem packing it nightly, and there was no other rock club anywhere close.

Bob had a big heart, and when he saw some homeless people hanging out in the parking lot, he did not call the police but had food brought out to them from the kitchen. Then in return, the homeless became eyes and ears for anything they saw in the lot.

CHAPTER 2

One Friday night, a new band was appearing, and it was an all-female band of five girls. These girls were extremely pretty, and the bouncers were always trying to hit on them, but house rules did not permit it although they tried. If the bouncers got caught, they would be fired. Some were pretty shrewd and did not get caught.

On a particular night, a nice-looking guy in his mid-twenties came in, looking for Bob. One of the front door guys went to get Bob to tell him there was some guy here to see him. Bob came to the front of the club and said, "You want to see me?"

This guy said, "Can we go somewhere to talk?"

Bob said, "Sure, come to my office." This guy introduced himself as Glenn and then asked Bob if he remembered a guy named Josh who worked here a long time ago. Bob said, "Sure I do. He was a great guy, funny, and became a cop. But I recently found out he was killed in a car crash, which really saddened me. I wanted to see if he wanted to come back in the club for a job." Glenn leaned forward in his chair and told Bob that he was Josh's son. Bob almost fell out of his chair and didn't know what to say. "You're really his son?"

Glenn said yes and asked if he could use another bouncer. Bob asked Glenn if he was working, and Glenn said, "Yes, I'm a deputy sheriff following in my dad's footsteps. So the job would only be on the weekends."

Bob asked, "Why do you want to, and won't it interfere in the police job?"

Glenn said, "I saw that the club reopened under the same name and wanted to see what my dad did so long ago. I think it is something I want to remember him by. And I see your plaque on the wall with his name on it, very nice—thank you for that.

Bob said, "OK, start this weekend and see me when you come back, but I also have to say there are no weapons allowed inside." Glenn said, "No problem." That Friday night after closing, Glenn asked Bob to come with him for a short ride. Bob said, "Sure where are we going?"

Glenn said, "You will know in a few minutes." They pulled up into a cemetery and walked to a fresh grave.

It was the grave of Josh. Bob was beyond tears and stood over the grave, thinking back about the old days. The headstone read "Sgt. Josh Scott, retired lawman, beloved husband, and father R.I.P." Glenn said, "I really miss him and his quick wit, which I inherited to my benefit."

Bob said, "I miss him also and thanks for taking me here." They then leave and not much is spoken on the way back.

On the following Monday, Bob had a phone message when he came to the office. The call was from Johnny Depp's publicist. He had an idea to have a two-day event show at the club, where Johnny would appear with his old band. The publicist said Johnny had a great time in the old place and thought he would showcase up-and-coming rock bands for the surrounding areas.

Later in the day, Bob called back the publicist and said, "Let's do it. We can schedule it in about a month, which gives time to advertise the two-day event and decide how much the cover will be." Bob told the publicist that he would have to have extra police coverage for both days. The publicist told Bob, "Johnny's production company will pay for the extra coverage."

Bob told him, "Johnny will be shocked to see someone who is here part-time. Let's set it for next month on the 15th."

The publicist told Bob, "That looks like a good date, pending any unforeseen problems, but Johnny is free that weekend."

Bob said, "I will fax over the contract by the end of the week, and if you can get the appropriate signatures and get it back quickly, things can move forward."

Later in the day, Bob got with Russ and told him of the two-day event, and Russ was crazy happy. Bob said, "As soon as I get the signed contract, you can get the advertising out and include radio, TV, and social media as well as setting up with Ticketmaster and the sheriff's office. I want at least ten deputies here both nights."

It was now the end of the week and the contract came back signed off and now all things were a go. Russ put the flyers together and got them out to all the media. This would have a lot of press coverage as there would be a lot of media camped out at the club, hoping to get a sound bite with Depp. The sheriff's office agreed to the ten deputies each night. Bob had to place larger orders of food and drinks to cover both nights and get more kitchen help as well as hiring a few more bouncers. These two nights would really put this club back on the map. Johnny's old band were notified, and all were in on the return to The Hurt. Bob told Russ to have a stretch limo ready to get Depp when he arrived at the airport. "I will have one of our staff be in the car to welcome Depp and his family and staff." Russ contacted a limo company and arranged for the limo on pickup night.

Bob was told by Russ that all the other bands had been contracted for the two-night event as well as the extra security needed. Bob was told by his vendors that they had his orders for food and drinks, and all were good; they would be delivered several days before the event. It was now Friday, the first night of the event. The limo was on the way to get Depp, the club was filling up with a long line of patrons to get in, the front-door security was bolstered by two deputies, and everyone was searched by hand and metal detection wand. The bars were busy serving drinks, and much food was being ordered; the servers on the floor were very busy and would probably have a great night in tips. The special lighting was operative, with background music playing from past recordings.

The crowd was very mixed. It looked like a bunch of wall Wall Street people that dressed down for the event. There were mostly women in the crowd along with many couples. The limo pulled up to the rear of the club, where a secure area was prepared for Depp and guarded by several deputies. Depp got out, carrying his guitar, and walked to the deputies, thanking them for his safety then walked into the building to the backstage area. He was met by Bob, who thanked him for being here, and Depp responded, "Thanks for the limo ride." Bob asked Depp to come to his office for a few minutes, which he did, telling his bodyguard he would be fine. When they walked into the office, Glenn was there, sitting on a couch. Bob told Johnny, "Here is someone I want you to meet. Remember Josh from the club back then, the guy who became a deputy sheriff?"

Johnny said, "Yes, I heard he was killed in a car crash."

Bob said, "This is Glenn, Josh's son who is also a deputy sheriff."

Johnny just sat there with his mouth open and said, "You look just like Josh." Johnny shook Glenn's hand and said, "Great to know you. Josh was a good guy and funny. He always kept me laughing. I was very sorry to hear about his death, and after all those years with the sheriff's office. It's a damn shame. Well, Bob, if it's OK with you, I want Glenn as my special guest tonight."

Bob said, "No problem," and Glenn thanked Johnny and got a picture with him.

Johnny then said, "Let me meet the band and get ready to go out."

Glenn and Bob said, "Great—see you out there." Glenn told Bob, "That was very cool, thank you." Then Glenn left the office to go out front.

Now the club was filled, and all was fine, so Bob got on stage and went to the microphone and started the intro for Johnny. He then said, "Ladies and gentlemen, it is my great privilege to introduce one of the past house bands from many years ago, with a special guest you all know from many movies, Johnny Depp and The Kids." The house went crazy as Johnny came out swinging like a teenager. The band played their oldies as Johnny played a mean guitar and sang.

After the first song, Johnny went to the mic and said, "I want to dedicate this night to an old friend who kept me laughing many years ago, a guy named Josh who is no longer with us and whose son is here tonight twenty-five years later. Josh, this is for you." As Glenn listened, he had tears running down his face.

After Johnny's music set was completed, he had to leave and get back to LA as he was only playing for one night. As Johnny went backstage moments later, he came back on stage for one encore song. He then thanked everyone and went to his limo and saw Glenn waiting near the limo. Johnny told Glenn, "It was great meeting you, and your dad was the best." He further stated, "When I do my next movie, I want you to be my personal guest on the set, and I will fly you out and put you up in a nice hotel, so here is my phone number and give me yours and I will call or one of my people will." Glenn thanked him, and Johnny was taken to the airport. The rest of the night went great, and Bob and Russ were very happy as were the servers, as they killed it in tips.

The second night went off without a hitch, but Bob was concerned with the two newer bouncers that took much interest in what Bob was doing during the night. Bob confronted them and asked, "Why are you so interested in watching me all night?" They said they wanted to learn what the boss did. Bob told them, "Just do your jobs and I'll do mine."

As the night came to an end, the club cleared out and the parking lot emptied. The sergeant in charge of the deputies' detail collected the check for their services, and Bob gave them a big thank you, telling them, "If you want to come to the club again off duty, just show your badge at the door, and there is no cover."

The sergeant said, "Thanks, I will tell them."

Now it was cleanup time, and there was a lot to clean up. Bob then went to his office and saw the two suspicious bouncers hanging around near the office. Bob told them to it was time for them to leave and go home. Bob was not comfortable with these two guys even after a background check.

Bob closed up shop until the next day and went home to get some rest. The next night, Bob went to the club to open for the night and saw a car out front with two guys in it, and it was the two suspicious bouncers. They were very early for work, and as Bob came up to them, he asked them, "Why are you here so early?" They told him, better early than late. Bob said, "That's nice, but you will have to wait out here for a while."

The guys said, "No problem." Then approximately an hour later, the doors opened, and the two guys went in and clocked in. They confronted Bob, asking why they had to wait so long.

Bob told them, "I was not ready to open, so next time, don't be too early."

Weeknights, the club was not that busy; there were the two house bands with a minimal crowd.

A disturbance broke out near the two newer bouncers, so they confronted the person causing the disturbance. This troublemaker pushed one of the bouncers as the other just stood by. They talked with the problem child, and they just got cursed at but did not respond. The guy got louder, making threats toward the bouncers. And again, they just stood there and took it. Bob witnessed this and walked over, as he saw the whole episode. He grabbed the problem by the shirt and dragged him out of the club, banning him. He told the bouncers at the door, "This guy is banned and does not come back in."

Bob then confronted the two bouncers who did nothing and told them that their poor performance was pathetic as bouncers and he couldn't have that here and fired them both. They started to disagree and argued with Bob, at which time Russ heard the argument and stepped in, telling them they had to leave, and a final paycheck would be sent to them. As they started to leave, they cursed out Bob and Russ. They were told that they were no longer allowed in the club.

Russ told the bouncers at the door that these two who were just dismissed were not allowed back in ever. Bob had flashbacks to the night of the homicide when threats were made as they were kicked out. Although Bob's rule was that no weapons were allowed in the club, Bob as well as Russ carried a pistol, but no one knew about it. Signs were posted outside the club, denoting no weapons allowed on the property.

CHAPTER 3

One tragic night at closing, Bob was accosted at gunpoint by a male subject asking for the money. Bob was by himself and armed with his pistol. The subject was pushing Bob to reopen and get the money, but as Bob opened the door, the subject took his eyes off Bob, at which time Bob spun around, pulling his pistol and shooting the subject several times, dropping him to the ground. Bob was not injured and called 911. Within minutes, numerous police were on scene along with medics, who pronounced the subject dead at the scene. Homicide detectives arrived and spoke with Bob, whom they knew. They had Bob go to his office and interviewed him, where they also learned that the front door was monitored by video.

Bob was able to play the tape and it was clearly seen that Bob acted in self-defense. The tape was a perfect witness. The tape was taken by the police as evidence as well as a taped statement from Bob. The medical examiner responded for the body. Bob called Russ and told him what happened and that he was fine. Bob told Russ that he would not be in the next day and to do the opening. Russ agreed and told Bob, "I'm glad you're OK." Bob said he would be home for a few days, thinking about what happened. Bob lived in a nice home in a gated community. He had a good-size yard for his dogs and a three-bedroom three-bath single-story home. He had lived in this home for many years. He was divorced for many years but had a girlfriend. His neighbors liked him a lot as he was always very friendly and accommodating.

Bob would play crime watch boss of the community and report any suspicious activity to the police, but there were never any issues. When Bob was walking his dogs one day, he saw a car parked just outside the gates and thought he recognized the driver as one of the two bouncers he had fired. Shrugging it off as it couldn't be, he just kept walking his dogs. One day later, he was getting many phone hang-ups. The phone would ring a few times then hang up. The caller ID came back as private. Bob blew it off as just the typical scam calls, we all get. While Bob went to the store, he left his dogs out in his yard in a fenced area. A short time later when he came home, he did not see his dogs as they always greeted him by the front near the gate. After Bob entered his house, he walked outside to the yard and saw his two dogs lying on the ground, not moving.

Bob quickly ran to them and discovered them to be dead. Bob lost it and started to cry out, causing his neighbors to come out to the commotion. Bob called the police, fearing foul play. When the police arrived, they told him initially that this was not a police matter but since they knew him and they were his friends, they checked into it. The police went door to door, asking if anyone had seen anyone suspicious in the area. At one home, the resident told the police of a suspicious car just outside the gate, occupied by a white male. After getting the description, they told Bob. Bob then told the police that it was the same car he saw outside the gate the other day, driven by someone he thought was one of the bouncers he fired earlier. Bob told the police he would go to the office and get the names of the two fired employees.

One of the officers followed Bob to retrieve the information. Later in the day, the police paid a visit to the bouncer's residence and in the driveway was the described vehicle. When questioned, the residents denied being near the home of Bob. Not having enough evidence of any wrongdoing, the police did a report as Bob brought his dogs to the vet's office for a necropsy. Bob was very distraught since he had his dogs for many years and he was recovering from just killing a bad guy. Bob called Russ and told him about his dogs, and Russ said, "Sorry to hear. Do you know what happened?"

Bob said, "Not yet, but I will soon."

About a week later, the vet called and told Bob, "I found poisoned meat in the dog, and that is the cause of death. I'm sorry."

Bob told the vet, "Thanks. I will take it from here."

Russ heard from Bob about the necropsy results and asked Bob, "So do you think those idiots did this?" Bob said yes but couldn't prove it. Russ told Bob to come over for dinner, and Bob said, "Fine."

During dinner, Bob told Russ, "Hire a few armed uniformed security people to patrol our parking lot when we are open, to keep an eye out for those two creeps."

Russ said, "We will have them here tonight and give them specific orders."

The following night, just prior to opening, Bob got word that two of his bouncers called in sick, so Bob called Glenn to see if he was available after work, and after being contacted, Glenn said, "Sure, I can come in, no problem." When Glenn finished work, he had to go home to change and put on the club T-shirt.

While Bob was in his office and Russ was checking on the sound equipment, the power to the building went out. Bob came out and found Russ asking what might have happened. Russ checked the circuit breakers, which are all tripped, then went outside to check the lines and discovered one of them was cut. Russ told Bob, and Bob called the police, thinking it was those two losers.

The police arrived at the club and took a report and photos of the damage. The police then went to the residence of the ex-bouncers and discovered they were not home. The police left their card to call them, but they never did.

Bob called an emergency electrician to fix the problem and have him cover the wires with a protective box that is locked on. Power was restored, and the club opened without any problems. The bouncers at the front door were given pictures of the ex-bouncers and were told these two guys were never permitted in the club or the parking lot, and the security guards outside had the same information.

It was a weeknight and the club was about half full, the band was playing, then a loud scream from the ladies' room. One of the female bouncers went into the ladies' room and found a girl unconscious in the stall. She called for assistance, and one of the guys came in to help carry the girl out. She was struggling to breathe as 911 was called.

Another girl came forward and said, "This is my girlfriend, and what happened?" She was asked if she took any drugs, and the friend said she did not know. Upon the paramedics' arrival, they gave her Narcan and she came to. She was then taken to the hospital in better condition. Bob heard about this and began to worry that this would happen often like it did so many years ago.

The club had been open for several weeks after the great opening with Johnny Depp. One of the outside security guards came in and asked to speak to Bob. When the guard met with Bob, he said, "My partner and I saw that one vehicle you told us about, and it had two people in it. The car drove in and then drove out."

Bob said, "Thanks for the information and for doing a good job." The guards then went back outside.

Russ checked in with Bob to make sure he was OK. Bob still had to deal with the judicial system after his shooting of the armed robber, whose family was suing Bob and the club for the death of their family member. The family felt that the killing over money was excessive and that Bob should have just given up the money. Bob questioned what world they were living in, but he had to get a lawyer and fight this ridiculous battle. Bob's lawyer knew this was just a money play by the decedent's family. Bob was not worried as he knew this was a bullshit lawsuit. The family really played it up on the stand, telling the jury the kid made a mistake and was planning on college after high school. Then it was Bob's turn on the stand.

Bob told the jury, "Was I supposed to get shot first if I did not respond?" He continued, stating he did not know this kid and did not know his alleged future. The defense attorney asked Bob how tall he was, and Bob said 6′8″.

"And how much do you weigh?"

Bob said about 300.

Then he was told, "The kid you shot was 5′8″ and about 160."

Bob said, "So what's your point? He had a big gun to back up his small stature."

The defense then said, "Judge, that's not responsive," and the judge told the jury to disregard the last comment. Bob was on the stand a short time and then the case went to the jury. They were out for approximately one hour. All were then called back into court for the verdict.

And to the great surprise of Bob, they awarded the decedent's family $100,000 in damages. Bob and his attorney almost fell off their chairs. It was believed that the size difference made the case. The award was against the club, not Bob, so the club's insurance had to pay. But then Bob told his attorney that they were appealing the verdict—that it was come to by morons. Months later on appeal, the verdict was overturned, and Bob and the club were not liable. After court, Bob celebrated at the club with the employees after work. Now at closing, Bob was not alone; he would always have another bouncer with him. Some of the bouncers were complaining about the wages they were paid. They were paid $20 per hour and were allowed two drinks for free after work if they wanted them.

This wage was one of the highest in the club business in the area. But now they wanted more, or they would leave and go elsewhere. There was one other club, a non-rock club that paid a little more per hour, but it was only open four nights per week, while The Hurt was open seven nights. So now came Friday night and the club was short six bouncers and Bob feared that the six decided to quit and go to the other club. Bob then withheld any money owed them until he found out what happened. Bob got in his car and drove over to the other club and found his bouncers there working. Bob confronted the club manager and found out that the six were just hired at the higher rate of pay. Bob spoke with several of the bouncers that had worked for him and told them that any money owed would not be forthcoming, because they quit.

CHAPTER 4

One of those bouncers got in Bob's face and said, "We will see about that," and Bob left and went back to his club. Bob immediately got with Russ and told him to hire more bouncers and complete background checks on them. Russ was very pissed off as to how those six guys just left without notice. Russ put out a job notice, and within a few days, he had more applicants than he could handle. He picked out ten and had backgrounds done on them. The next day, they started and seemed to be doing well. The following Saturday night, several of the bouncers that left came into the club, looking for Bob. As they were kept inside near the front door, Bob came from his office and confronted the ex-employees.

They said they wanted their last paycheck, and Bob said, "Sorry, no, you cost me money by leaving, so we are even." Then one of the ex-employees pushed Bob, which was not a good thing to do. They were never informed that Bob held four different black belts in different types of martial arts, and at 6'8″ and 300 pounds, he could really hurt you. Bob told this guy to not touch him, so the guy pushed Bob again. Then Bob grabbed this guy and put him to sleep, at which time several of the others jumped in, but Bob swept the floor with them. The bouncers working the front door called 911 about a fight as well as having the paramedics respond. Then the cops put cuffs on Bob for causing a disturbance.

He was taken to the police station and charged with disorderly conduct as well as the others when they got out of the hospital. Bob needed to be careful because if he got arrested on a felony charge, he could lose his liquor license. Luckily, he was charged with a misdemeanor. At the police station, Bob was given a notice to appear (NTA), so he did not go to jail. Approximately one month later, he had his court appearance along with the others involved. The judge saw the size difference and saw that it was three against one and tossed out the charge against Bob. The other three were found guilty and did not look too good. Bob was beginning to think that buying the club was not such a good idea, but then after thinking about it, felt it was in fact a great idea. He always had flashbacks to the look on Laura's face when he did something and that made him smile.

Bob got a long-distance call from Los Angeles one night and it was Johnny Depp's publicist. He called to tell Bob that Johnny loved being back at the club where he started and wanted to make a return engagement, but this time with his own band. Bob said, "Absolutely. When is he interested in coming?" Bob was told, "Possibly in approximately five to six weeks after a movie shoot he is on." Bob said, "Of course we would love to have him back. Just get me a more confirmed date, and I will send out the contract."

The publicist said, "Fine and thank you, and by the way, we know more security is involved, and we will pay for it." Bob got with Russ and told him the news, which made Russ smile from ear to ear.

Bob said, "We will get a firm date soon, so you can get the advertising out and it will be a one-night play only." Now about a week later, Bob got the confirmed date from LA, and he sent the contract. He then told Russ, "Get the advertising out, and we will have a packed house. Also contact the sheriff's office that we will need ten deputies for the event and will get the contract from them. Also notify our vendors for extra drinks and food."

Now the event was here, and the club was packed, knowing that Johnny Depp was back. The club picked him and his group up from the airport via a limo and brought them to the club. Upon his arrival, he met with the deputies backstage, took pictures and signed autographs, and then went inside to see Bob. Johnny asked about Glenn and if he was here, and Bob said, "Sorry, no, he is working the streets tonight, but I told him you are back, and he will try to make an appearance." The show started, and Johnny was introduced along with his band. He played for about an hour and took a break then back for another hour. He did great and the patrons loved it. After his set, he came into the audience and to a secure table on the second floor, facing the stage. He was there with his bodyguard and some of his band, along with Bob and Russ. They all posed with Johnny for some photos and then sat there watching the house band.

Some patrons came up to the table and were permitted pictures and autographs. Several overzealous fans tried to grab at Johnny but were quickly removed away from him and escorted out of the club without incident. At the end of the night, Johnny had to leave and told Bob thanks for another great night. Bob told him, "Anytime you want to return, just call."

Johnny told Bob, "I have a birthday coming up in about ten months and I may want to have my party here and rent out the entire club for my friends and family, so I will let you know."

Bob said, "Terrific, thanks, Johnny, and have a nice flight," and with that, Johnny and his group exited and thanked the deputies again and left for the airport. It was a banner night for all. The servers made great tips, and the club got a great review online and in the local paper.

Now the club was getting ready to close, and everyone was cleaning up. Once all was cleaned, it was time for everyone to have their drinks and go home. At closing, Bob and another bouncer locked up and departed. It was now approximately 4:00 a.m., and Bob was in bed, trying to get some well-deserved sleep. At approximately 5:00 a.m., there was a loud crash, and Bob got up and grabbed his gun. He then heard a car roar out of the area. A rock was thrown through the front window, with a note attached. The note basically said, "Watch your back." Bob called 911 and made a report with the police and asked them for a special watch due to the increase in incidents. So each night for several staggered hours, a police car would be in the area. Bob felt good about this, and hopefully, he could get a decent night's sleep. The following morning, Bob called Russ and told him about the rock incident. Russ told Bob to stay with him for a while if he wanted, but Bob refused.

Bob felt a little skeptical on how Russ processed the information on the violent issue, so he kept a closer eye on him. Although Russ was like Bob's right-hand man, there was a little jealousy.

The following night at opening, Russ told Bob all was good for the open, meaning the lighting and sound. Then Bob walked by Russ as he was on his cell phone. Bob thought he overheard Russ telling someone to get it done right. Bob did not know what Russ was talking about and moved on. What Bob did not know was that Russ was planning a violent disturbance in the club in an attempt to take over the ownership. Russ knew all the troubles Bob had already incurred and was teetering on losing his liquor license, which would then fold up the club. But then, Bob was approached by another bouncer who was good friends with Bob and was told of the problem Russ was attempting to make. Bob couldn't believe it as he thought of Russ like a brother. Bob then called Russ into the office and confronted Russ on what he had heard.

At first, Russ denied any wrongdoing, so Bob called in the Mike the bouncer who had found out about the issue. Mike then spelled out what Russ was up to. Bob felt very betrayed and told Russ, "I don't know what to say but you're out, and when your friends come in to start trouble, they will be out too." Russ was escorted out with a trespass warning and told not to return. If and when Bob decided to sell it wouldn't be to Russ, he guaranteed it. A short time later, a few guys came in and started to bother people, and they were swiftly dealt with and tossed out. Mike, who overheard the conversation, had become close with Bob and promoted to Russ's position as floor manager in charge of the lighting and sound. Mike was very thankful and told Bob he would always have his back.

Luckily, Mike had some experience in his new position as he took up stage lighting in college but still needed to learn the sound part of the job. Bob was able to educate Mike quickly in the sound department. Mike was a big burly guy that you would not want to mess with, so when there were no lighting or sound issues, he stepped in as a bouncer. Mike was mindful that he could not afford any major drug issues in the club or Bob would lose his liquor license. He hired a private security K-9 drug detection dog to stand guard at the front door, and if the dog alerted to someone, he or she would be questioned and searched. If they did not adhere to the request, they were denied entry.

This became costly for Bob as it was coming out of the club's profits, but it was worth it. Bob got to see the dog in action one night. A group of couples were coming, when the dog alerted to one of the men coming in. The guy was stopped and questioned and then asked to empty his pockets as the dog alerted to a narcotic. The guy started to sweat and pulled out a small baggie of cocaine. The guy was given an opportunity to dump it or leave, and the police would not be called. The guy decided to dump it and then was admitted in. He thanked them for not calling the police, but his girlfriend was very pissed off. She yelled at him, "You do cocaine?" He yelled back, "Fuck off!" She then turned around and said, "You're an asshole. Take me home." So they both left. Who knows what happened with them?

One early Friday night, two men in suits came to the club unannounced, asking to see the owner. They were told to wait a minute while they got Bob. Bob came to the front and greeted the two men. They identified themselves as IRS agents. Bob brought them to his office and was told that they were informed of some irregularities in the books. Bob asked where this came from and was told that it was confidential. Bob assumed that Russ made a bogus complaint to get back at him. Bob knew all was on the up and up, but the IRS can make your life miserable. They asked to see his books and any financial paperwork involving the club. Bob said that he did not have everything here and he would have to get it from the bank.

Well, the agent told Bob that they went to his bank with a warrant and retrieved all his financial paperwork for the club and his personal finances. The agent told Bob, "This investigation will take a while, so until then, you have to shut down the operation."

Bob asked, "How long, as this will put people out of work and hurt my business." He was told it should take a few weeks at most. Bob had to agree and saw the two agents out. Bob then gathered his employees and told them, "The IRS received a complaint about the finances surrounding the club, and until their investigation ends, I have to shut down."

Bob told them all, "I am very sorry for the inconvenience, and as soon as I get the OK to reopen, I will have you all back if you want to come back. But let me tell you I have a good feeling who made the complaint and I will deal with him."

Now that the club was closed, pending the outcome of the IRS investigation, Bob decided to ask his longtime girlfriend to marry him. He set up the scene at a nice restaurant, and after being seated, he proposed. He showed her the ring, and she said, "Hell yes, I will marry you." Bob put the ring on her finger and kissed her. They then enjoyed a great meal. Bob told her about the IRS investigation, and she told him, "Don't worry. You did nothing wrong." After the meal was over, they went home for some alone time.

A few days later, Bob was called down to the federal building where the IRS was located. Upon his arrival, he was met by the two agents working the case. They all sat in a large conference room and laid out numerous pieces of paper showing many financial transactions that were a little suspicious. They told Bob that he should get a criminal attorney because it looked like their findings would go to the grand jury. Bob just sat there in silence, thinking what could be criminal and when all this would end already; it had been one thing after another. Bob now had to get a criminal defense lawyer, which is costly. Bob found one and needed to come up with $10,000 as a retainer, which he did. He told his fiancée about this, and she was now very concerned.

The IRS sent their investigation to the grand jury, and after fifteen hours, they came back with a true bill, meaning indictment. The IRS agents called Bob's attorney and told him about the indictment and told the attorney to have Bob at the IRS office at 9:00 a.m. to turn himself in. The attorney said OK and called Bob to tell him. Bob was afraid of going to prison for an unknown problem. The next day, Bob and his attorney responded to the IRS office, where he turned himself in; he was then handcuffed and taken to booking. After booking he was given a bail of $50,000, of which he needed 10 percent. Bob posted his bail and was taken home by his attorney. Bob was in rough shape mentally now that he had the IRS after him and problems at the club and with some past employees.

The club now had been closed for over a month, and Bob was on trial for financial crimes. Bob's attorney had received all the information from the feds and discovered that Bob was not upfront about everything. It appeared that Bob had been running illegal guns through the club and showing the transactions through the club's finances. Many of the weapons were automatic weapons, and Bob did not have a federal firearms license, which now brought in the ATF. Bob started this endeavor in selling weapons to help with some financial issues he was having. After several weeks, it was time for the trial, and after about two more weeks, Bob was found guilty and sentenced to five years in prison.

Bob's fiancée was devastated and told Bob that she would take care of things at the club. Bob said, "With this felony conviction, there is no way I can keep my liquor license, so put the club up for sale even if I have to take a loss." Bob further said that he felt bad for his employees. When the club went up for sale, the first person to come forward with interest was Russ, the guy who started this mess. Bob's fiancée told Bob, and he gave in, saying, "Just get rid of it." Russ was contacted, and she took the offer for purchase. After dealing with the lawyers regarding the club changing hands, Russ took ownership and called back the employees that were let go.

Russ even called back the two bouncers that Bob had fired, but Russ was unaware of the problems they gave Bob. Now that Bob was out of the picture for now, Russ had to take the lead and repair any damage that was done to the club's finances. Russ was happy that he had Johnny Depp coming back in a few months for a birthday bash and renting the entire club, but then Johnny heard what happened to Bob and how Russ had his hand in it. Johnny and his publicist did not like how things went down, so he cancelled his birthday bash at the club. Russ was devastated because he would have really cleaned up that one night. Russ tried to plead with Johnny's publicist, but it was to no avail. Russ was always bragging about how he got the club from Bob, but most could not care less about it.

Many bouncers in the club really did not like Russ but liked working the club. Glenn showed up one Saturday night and asked for Bob. Russ came out to meet Glenn and tell him that Bob was a little shady and that he was in federal prison for a few years for financial crimes. Glenn couldn't believe it, so he went to see Bob at the prison. While Glenn was at the prison, Bob told him how he wound up in the prison. Glenn could not believe that Russ would do this, but he did. Russ now had to come up with a new angle to get people in, so he decided to have amateur stripper night. He had stripper poles installed on stage and advertised for each Friday, women twenty-one and over could compete in a stripper pole contest for a $500 prize. The advertising went out, and it brought in many girls and plenty of guys.

CHAPTER 5

Glenn had put the word out to his fellow deputies about what Russ did to Bob, so when the club needed to hire security, no deputies would take the job and the local police were not allowed to work at clubs. Russ had to get a security company for security coverage, and if there was an issue, then the police would be called out. Russ really didn't like this arrangement as he liked having the cops working the club. The two bouncers that were fired by Bob when he had the club were becoming troublemakers; they turned out to be bullies always looking for any reason to fight with someone, until one night they picked on the wrong guy. They saw this guy cursing at the waitress, and when they walked over just to tell him to stop his verbal attacks, these bouncers went to grab him by the arm.

The guy pulled back and said, "Don't touch me." The patron then said, "I'm leaving." The bouncers then pushed him a little to make him leave faster. Not knowing this guy was an MMA champion fighter, they both got their clock cleaned by this guy. Just after he laid the two bouncers out, he was jumped on by several other big bouncers and subdued and held for the cops. The two bouncers thought they could push everyone around until they met their match. The two suffered broken jaws and missing teeth and were taken to the hospital. The two would now be out of work for a few months. The MMA guy went to jail on aggravated battery charges.

Now the club was down two bouncers, so Russ talked to the security personnel outside and offered two of the biggest a bouncing job temporarily. So now these two new bouncers started the next night but did not get a background check. They showed up and got a few minutes of training and a uniform shirt. Toward the end of the night, the cashier at the front of the club needed a break and asked one of these new guys to watch the booth for a few minutes. When the cashier came back, she continued to take in cash for entrance fee. At the end of the night, she counted the money and was short over $100. She remembered the only time she left was to take a short break, leaving one of the new bouncers in the booth.

She told Russ, and he confronted the bouncer in question. He denied taking any cash and emptied his pockets and took off his shoes, no cash. So now the cashier was responsible for the loss and had to pay from her own pocket. At the end of the night, she was very pissed off and confronted the bouncer who gave the break. She got in his face and said, "You took the money, I know you did." He denied it and left to go home. A few days later, Russ got the background check back on the two new guys and was shocked to see that the one that gave the cashier her break had a theft history. He knew this was his fault, and he told the cashier that she was not responsible for the missing money and that he fired that one bouncer. She now felt relieved.

Months went by and the two injured bouncers return and have a meeting with Russ about their bullying approach to people and that it had to stop. They said they would change their ways and not push anyone around. Bob's fiancée visited him often, knowing that when he got out, they would get married. But she was spending a lot of time with Russ at the club. Russ always had a thing for her but could never make a move when Bob was around. But when she was in the club, she would wink at Russ every time she walked by him. While she was visiting Bob, he asked about the club. He was curious how Russ was running things. Bob asked her to go by once in a while just to see what was happening; she agreed and would report back to Bob. But now that Bob had been locked away for a while, she started to think about her personal needs such as sex.

So she went to the club and had a drink and waited for Russ to meet her. When he showed up, he sat very close to her and put his hand on her open legs. She asked how the club ownership was coming along. Russ says, "Come to the office where it is quieter." Once in the office, they started passionately kissing as Russ ran his hand under her dress. She then ran her hand over his zipper area, caressing his penis, which was getting hard. She removed his belt and undid his pants and they fell to the floor. He then hiked up her dress and turned her around and had her lean over the desk. He got behind her and went inside her from the back. After a few minutes, he withdrew and turned her around, facing him.

She got on her knees and got a mouthful of DNA. After they finished, they got dressed, and she left the club. On the way out, Russ asked her, "Will I see you soon?"

She said, "Maybe." On the way out of the club, she stared at one of the nicer-looking built bouncers and licked her lips. Since Bob had been in prison, his fiancée had become the club whore. She left the club and went to her car, where she wrote down her phone number on a piece of paper, and came back to the front door and gave the number to the bouncer. She then went home, and at approximately 3:00 a.m., she got a call from the bouncer asking what she was doing, she told him, "You, if you want to come over."

He told her, "In about fifteen minutes," then hung up. The bouncer arrived and was met at the door by Bob's fiancée in a see-through nightie. He came in and immediately started going at it. In a matter of minutes, he was undressed, and she was on her knees, giving him oral sex. Then they went onto the bed, where they banged away for hours. When finished, he got dressed and left. She went to bed as she was to visit Bob later in the day.

Now later in the day, she visited Bob, who told her that she looked tired. She told him that she could not sleep because he was locked up. Bob asked about Russ and the club. She told him all was well, and Russ seemed to have things in hand. Bob then asks if the same crew is there. She smiled and said, "Yes, thankfully." After about an hour, she left, telling Bob she would be back at the end of the week.

The next day, one of the bouncers, named Steve, came to see Bob, who was thrilled to see one of the guys he had hired. Steve told Bob that he couldn't wait for him to get out and put all this behind. He then said that he had some disturbing information about Bob's fiancée but was afraid to say anything. Bob asked, "What is it? Just say it."

"Bob, your fiancée has been cheating on you, and I have proof."

Bob said, "You are kidding," and asked for the proof.

Steve told him, "Last week, she came in to see Russ and she was in the office a long time, then as she was leaving, she was making sexy eye contact with one of the guys at the front door. She then went to her car and came back to give her phone number to him and he took it."

Bob asked who the bouncer was. Steve said, "It's Alan."

Bob said, "That son of a bitch, wait till I get out." Steve then showed his phone to Bob, as he had pictures of some of the encounter. Bob said, "Can you send that one to her?"

Steve said, "Yes, what is the number?" Bob gave him her phone number, and the picture of her and the bouncer getting the phone number was sent.

Bob thanked him and said, "I won't forget this." Steve then left and went to the club to start work.

Later in the evening, Bob's fiancée called Alan and told him, "I got a picture of us at the club where I gave you my phone number. I'm sure Bob knows, and he will go out of his mind, as I'm sure someone showed him. We cannot see each other anymore, sorry. Goodbye."

A few days later, Bob's fiancée came to see him as if nothing was going on. As they sat together in the visiting room, Bob asked how she was, and she said, "Fine, and I miss you."

Bob said, "Really? I heard you have been a very busy girl with Russ and Steve at the club. I know all about your antics since I've been in here. Sleeping with Russ and then Steve in the same day, you are a fucking whore. Take that ring off. We are through, so now you can go to the club a free woman to bang whomever you want."

She told Bob that she was sorry. "It was just an impulse move and I'm sorry."

Bob said, "You cannot control your impulses. You sicken me. Now get the fuck out of here."

Bob was very pissed off and now felt that he needed to do his time and then settle the score at a later time.

Back at the club, a few weeks later, a woman came in, asking for Russ. One of the guys at the door called Russ and told him, "A woman is here to see you."

He told the bouncer, "Escort her to my office." The bouncer told the woman to follow him to the office. She knocked on the door and he opened it. She stepped in and closed the door behind her. Then multiple shots rang out. She then came out very calmly and left the club. At this time, no one heard the shots because of the loud music, but when Russ had not been seen for a while, Mike went to the office and found Russ shot multiple times, dead on the floor.

He came running out, not knowing what to do, so he finally called 911 and the police and crime scene unit showed up. The club was emptied except for the employees. A homicide detective talked with the bouncers and discovered that they saw an unknown woman come in, asking for Russ, then escorted her into the office, where she stayed for a few minutes until she left the club. She casually walked out into the parking lot to her car. The detective asked if a car was seen and was told no. The front-door bouncer who escorted her to the office gave a description of a white female about 5'7", 110 lbs., short brown hair, wearing a white T-shirt and jeans, and carrying a black purse. The detective thanked him and then went to the office, where he found Russ's cell phone.

The detective scrolled through it and found several female names and phone numbers. He was able to cross-reference the numbers to an address. Then he and his partner started to track down the women. After their third check, they found a woman fitting the description given by the bouncer. The detectives asked if she knew Russ, and they were told, "Yes, I'm his wife." She then asked what was wrong. She was told that a female shot and killed Russ earlier at the club. They then asked where she was earlier, and they were told that she just got home from being out of town.

They then asked if there was anyone that would want to hurt Russ. She said Bob, as he was the club owner prior and felt that he was imprisoned because of Russ: "Bob is in federal prison now and blames Russ for being there." The detectives then asked where she was, and they were told, "Just the next city over, in Fort Lauderdale." The detectives then asked where she stayed and were told, "a friend's home." They said, "OK, we will need the name and address." She said no problem and gave the information to them. They said thank you and left. She then immediately called her friend to make sure she backed her story.

The detectives felt she was now a person of interest and got a search warrant for her car and home. They called for a uniformed cop to stand by the residence until they got the warrant. As the detective left, the uniform saw the woman come out and go into the trunk and pull out a black plastic garbage bag and put it in a neighbor's trash can; she then went back inside.

A short time later, the one detective returned with the warrant as the other detective went to see the friend in Fort Lauderdale. The detective got with the uniform, who told him that the suspect came out and took a black garbage bag out and put it in the neighbor's trash can. The detective went and retrieved the bag and discovered a blood-splattered T-shirt. He then went to the car and found what appeared to be blood on the driver's seat. The car was secured, and the female was arrested on suspicion of murder. As the cuffs were put on her, she blurted out, "He deserved it. He was cheating on me after all I did for him." She told the detective, "I will give a statement because I did it." He asked where the gun was, and he was told it was in the house in a kitchen drawer. He retrieved it and then went to the office with the suspect.

Since the arrest of Russ's wife, the club went into a receivership and the doors were locked. Bob heard of the mayhem and the club being locked up after the arrest. Bob did not feel sorry for Russ or his wife since he was caught cheating with Bob's fiancé. Then Bob got a visit from Glenn and things started to change. Glenn told Bob that he was interested in buying the club and he wanted Bob involved in the day-to-day operations and the liquor license would be in Glenn's name. Glenn told Bob that he and several other deputies wanted to invest in the club and keep it open for rock and roll's sake. Bob did not know what to say except thanks to all. Glenn and his investors went through all the red tape and finally got the club and brought back most of the employees.

They made some changes like getting rid of the stripper poles and changing the food and drink menu. And since cops were owners now, the background checks were more thorough and not rushed. The only problem the new owners had was patrons coming in and noticing the new police owners and remembering them from a past arrest. But all who came in were searched for weapons and alcohol, as well as having the drug detection K-9 out front. Glenn got rid of the armed security for the parking lot and hired off-duty deputies through the agency for outside protection. This made Glenn more comfortable and those who worked the club got fed on the house.

Since Glenn took over, he was able to get in contact with Johnny Depp's agent and publicist in an effort to have him reschedule his birthday bash here at the club. A few days later, Glenn got a call from the publicist, and Johnny agreed to come back for the birthday ever since he heard that Glenn was the new owner. Now that the party was back on schedule, Glenn had to start planning well in advance, from food and drink to extra security and bouncers. He knew that this would be a big media event, so he hired a maintenance crew to clean up outside and paint where necessary. Hollywood-style searchlights would also be brought in and set up in the parking lot. Glenn also received word from MTV that they wanted to film the party, but that would have to be OK with Depp's people.

Back at the prison, Bob had read about Depp holding his birthday at the club and was happy for Glenn. Fast-forward to the event and Johnny's invited guests were showing up in limos and fancy cars. Luckily, Glenn set up for valet service. Johnny was not there yet as he was en route from the airport. The extra deputies were waiting for him to arrive at the rear of the club, which was a more secure location than the front of the club. Upon his arrival, he met the deputies and thanked them for their service and told them he will take pictures at the end of the night. Johnny then came into the club via a back door and met Glenn. They hugged and Johnny told Glenn he was glad Glenn was the new club owner.

This night, Johnny was not on stage but with his friends and family just listening to the house bands, but then he decided to jump on stage and grab a guitar and play, the crowd went wild. The club was packed, and the servers were making bank and happy to work hard. At the end of the night, which was three o'clock the next morning, the club started to clear out, and the valet parkers were killing it on tips. As Johnny was getting ready to leave, he thanked Glenn for a great time and then went out for pictures with the cops. He then departed with his family. Now was time to clean up, and the employees were finding empty baggies of cocaine and suspicious pills on the ground as well as money, ID cards, and jewelry. Most of the items found were put in the club's lost and found.

When all was done, Glenn went home to relax and get some sleep as he had the next day off. The following day, Glenn just caught up on household chores: mowing the lawn, a little outside house painting, and cleaning his police car. He was having some friends over for a barbecue lunch and beers. Glenn's house was a three-bedroom two-bath with a two-car garage and pool. He had lived there for a few years with his two beagle dogs. He had a girlfriend that was a nurse at a local hospital.

When the friends started to arrive for lunch, they asked how his girlfriend Susan was. Glenn said, "She is still at the hospital and should be here soon."

Now the barbecue was going, and the beers were flowing, and Susan arrived home. She told all that she would change and be right back and told Glenn, "Have a beer ready for me, please." When Susan came back, they started talking about the night-before craziness at the club.

She told Glenn that several overdoses came in late in the morning and told the doctors they got the cocaine at the club, from one of the bouncers. Glenn said, "What? Did they say which bouncer it was or a description? This is all I need, a drug dealer working at the club, which is owned by cops." He continued, "I have to find out who it is and set him up and soon. Are the patients still in the hospital?" Susan said yes. Glenn said, "I will go see them later. What room are they in?" Glenn got the information, and several hours later, he left the lunch and went to see the patients in the hospital. He was told they were two females. Glenn got to the hospital and met the girls in their room. He identifies himself as a deputy sheriff and the club owner. The girls seemed fairly lucid and agreed to talk.

They were asked if they remembered which bouncer they got the cocaine from. They told Glenn they did not know his name, but he was tall and muscular with dark hair and short beard. Glenn immediately knew who they were talking about and thanked the girls. He did tell them, "If you come back to the club looking for drugs, you will go to jail, so make better decisions next time and remember where you are now because of that choice."

Glenn called his narcotics sergeant and told him the story and wanted to set the guy up with some undercover females. Glenn got the OK from the narcotics sergeant and would send in several undercover females this Friday night. Glenn thanked him and went back to his lunch. Now it was Friday night, and he was contacted by the narcotics sergeant and given the description of the two undercover females.

The sergeant staged outside with a few of his detectives. The club was getting packed, and the bouncer in question was there and working the upstairs section where it was a little darker. The bands were playing, people were dancing. The undercover female and her friend watched the bouncer from a distance to see if he was selling anything, but it was dark, so they had to get a closer look, and when they did, they saw a couple of hand-to-hand exchanges. So they made their move and walked up to him. They first started by making small talk and then asked if there was anything around to make the night better. The bouncer first said, "There's me." They said maybe but not tonight; it was kind of a girls-only night. The bouncer then said, "What exactly are you looking for?" and they told him, "a little pick-me-up for us to party with."

He showed them a small plastic baggie with a white powdery substance. They said, "How much?" and he said $20. One of the undercover females said, "OK, is it good?" He told them hell yes. She handed him a marked $20 bill and said thanks then walked away. She then took the baggie out to one of the detectives in the parking lot for it to be tested, and it showed positive for cocaine. The detectives and the sergeant now came into the club and asked for Glenn. They told him they had the bouncer on possession and delivery of cocaine. They asked if Glenn could escort him to the front door so they didn't have a big problem in the club.

Glenn got with the bouncer and told him he needed him at the front and walked with him there. The bouncer was met by the detective and then handcuffed and told what he was charged with. Glenn told him, "I cannot believe you would do this here. You're done. Take him the hell out of here." The other bouncers at the door were then told what the guy did, and Glenn made it clear that if you were doing anything illegal in his club, you would go to jail. The rest of the night went very smoothly.

Glenn was very grateful that his girlfriend told him about the drug use, so he bought her an expensive day at a spa. So later in the day, he presented it to her, and she loved it and gave him a big kiss. A few days later, Susan went to the spa for the day and was getting her massage in a back room when she and the masseuse heard a big commotion up front. There was a lot of screaming and items being broken.

Susan and the masseuse stepped out from the room, and a guy in a face mask saw them and recognized Susan as the girlfriend of Glenn. He then produced a gun and yelled out to her, "This is for Glenn." He fired off one round into Susan, and she fell to the ground. Others in the spa started yelling as the gunman fled.

Susan was tended to as 911 was called. Meanwhile, others were trying to stop the bleeding and keep her as calm as possible. Susan then told the manager to call her boyfriend as he was a cop. Glenn was at work on patrol not too far from the spa when he got a call from the spa manager. She told him, "There has been an accident and Susan is injured and she wanted me to call you." He then radioed in that there was an incident at the spa to dispatch just as they dispatched him to the call. He now heard that the incident was a shooting with a female victim. He was also told by dispatch that the paramedics are already en route. Back at the spa, Susan was near death and told the manager, "Tell Glenn what the gunman said and that I love him." She then succumbed to her injury just as Glenn arrived.

He was in a panic, and even with all his training, he did not know what to do. He was freaking out and crying, yelling out no, no, no. The medics arrived and saw Susan was dead and pronounced her. They got a sheet and covered her up as detectives and the crime scene unit started to arrive. Glenn was taken away by fellow deputies who also knew Susan and tried to comfort him. He then heard what the gunman said before shooting and thought this was tied in to having the bouncer arrested for dealing cocaine. He told this to the homicide detectives, and they looked into it. The body was then removed by the ME for autopsy.

Glenn got out of work early and called Susan's family, who lived out of state. Glenn did not how to tell them their only child was murdered. But he got the courage to tell them, and all he then heard was screaming on the other end.

Then he was asked what happened and he told them. They told Glenn they would be down as soon as possible and hung up. Glenn was now home and had to plan a funeral. A few days later, Susan's family was down and getting ready for the funeral. A funeral home was chosen along with a casket. Susan was Catholic, so she had a Catholic mass. After the mass, she was taken to the cemetery with a sheriff's escort. At the grave site, the priest said a few words and then she was lowered into her grave. Glenn felt responsible as he sent her to the spa for a nice day. But he firmly believed that the guy he had arrested had something to do with the shooting, and he vowed to find out.

CHAPTER 6

A few days after the funeral, Glenn checked on the whereabouts of the guy he had arrested. The jail records showed that he had been released before the fatal shooting. Glenn then got with the homicide detectives working the case and briefed them on the history between this guy and him The detective advised Glenn that they would get a search warrant on the guy's home and car and then interview him, and if anything turned up, they would notify Glenn. Meanwhile, Glenn did a shadow investigation on his own, which was against the department policy. But first he started to pack up Susan's personal belongings as her parents wanted them. There really wasn't much: some clothes, personal items, and a laptop computer. The parents took all the possessions and went back home.

The next day, Glenn started to get visitors from the hospital Susan worked at. Each person that came over was in tears and consoled Glenn; they stayed a short time and left. The next day, Glenn got a call from one of the homicide detectives, telling him that the suspect was not around and might have left town. They executed the search warrant but found nothing incriminating, and since there was no car, they could not serve the search warrant. But then the detectives got a call from a shop owner near the spa, stating that he was checking his video camera and saw a suspicious car parked just a few doors down from the spa and a muscular white male jump in it and take off quickly. The car was described as dark-colored two-door Ford Mustang, and the detectives said, "That is the same car the suspect has."

So they put out a BOLO (be on the lookout) on that vehicle countrywide with a description and a comment that he was a suspect in a homicide. If stopped, proceed with caution; he is armed and dangerous. Hopefully this guy would not ditch the car and get a different one. But as we know, life goes on, and Glenn went back to the club. He brought in one of his coworkers from the agency to fill in as a bouncer on weekends. The activity at the club was moving along without any issues, and for months, people were having a good time and the servers were making money. Then Glenn got a call from one of the homicide detectives that the suspect in the shooting was captured in Georgia after a brief police chase. He was in the same car, and a gun was also recovered, which was believed to be the one used in the homicide. The suspect was fighting extradition and would be several months before he came down to stand trial. Glenn was happy to hear this information and could not wait for the trial to start.

Now a few months later, all the trial prep work was done, and it was time to start the trial. Glenn was subpoenaed for his testimony and was in his sheriff's uniform. After a few preliminary witnesses, Glenn was called to the stand. He was sworn in and he took his seat. The prosecutor asked him to state his name and profession, which he did, then on to the questioning.

Are you the owner of the club called The Hurt?
Yes.

Did you hire Mr. Jones as a bouncer?
Yes.

Do you see him in the courtroom today?
Yes, that's him there with a brown suit.

Did you have the opportunity to dismiss him from his position at the club?
Yes.

What was the reason?
He was selling cocaine to the patrons.

Was Mr. Jones arrested?
Yes.

By whom?
The sheriff's office narcotics unit.

How was the arrest made?
Glenn said that he got in contact with the narcotics unit sergeant, and they sent in two undercover female detectives to make a buy, which they did. He was then brought to the front of the club and handcuffed and booked.

After the arrest, have you seen Mr. Jones?
No.

Your honor, no further questions.
Defense, you're up.

Good morning, deputy.
Good morning, sir.

I just have a few questions. How long have you owned the club?
Almost one year.

When you hired my client, did you interview him?
Yes.

Did you have a background check done?
Yes.

Isn't it true that the only reason you focused on my client was because he was dealing drugs in the club?
No. Just that after I was informed about the shooting, I felt it had to be him because of him saying on the way out of the spa, "This is for Glenn."

No further questions.
Now the defense called Mr. Jones to the stand. The bailiff swore him in, and he sat down.

Mr. Jones, did you work at The Hurt?
Yes.

What was your position at the club?
I was a bouncer.

On the night in question, were you arrested for selling cocaine to a female undercover deputy?
Yes.

Did the owner then fire you from the club?
Yes.

The night Susan Clark was shot and killed, where were you?
I was at home.

Is there anyone that can corroborate that?
No, I was alone.

Did you want to get back at the club owner for your arrest?
No, I was an idiot just trying to make extra money, and I'm sorry.

Your honor, nothing further. I submit that there is no witness, no DNA, nothing to put my client at the shooting scene and request this charge be dismissed.
The judge then asked the prosecutor if there was any further evidence, and he replied, "Not at this time." The judge then said, "I

have to dismiss this case at this time, and if there is any further evidence that is discovered, you are allowed to retry the case. Court is dismissed."

As the defendant walked out of the courtroom, he leaned over and said to Glenn, who was still seated, "I miss her." Glenn got up as if he was going to attack Mr. Jones but resisted. Glenn then got up and left with several of his friends that were with him. They then went to the club to have a drink and food.

Fast-forward a few years and Glenn got a call from Bob from prison, telling him that he was getting out in a week and wanted to see him. Glenn said, "Great, of course, get me a time and exact date, and I will have someone pick you up."

Bob said, "Thanks, I will." After a few weeks, Bob was released, and a car from the club was there to pick him up. He was first taken to his home that he once shared with his fiancée; now a free and unattached man, he was a little sad but very happy too.

He dropped off his belongings and then was taken to the club. As he walked in, he was greeted by Glenn, and they gave each other a big hug. They both went back to the office and talked business. Bob told Glenn that he had interest in becoming the owner again. Glenn told him that he and several other deputies had a shared ownership. Bob said, "I will make you an offer, and I would like to keep you as a partner because I cannot get the liquor license."

Glenn said, "I will talk with the other owners, and I have a feeling they will want out."

Bob said, "Thanks. Can I get a beer?" Glenn said sure, and they shared a beer.

A few days went by, and Glenn called Bob and told him, "The other owners advised they will sell their share, and we can get the paperwork done over the next few days."

Bob came up with the funds and bought out the other owners, and now Bob was the majority owner with Glenn. They decided to have a special night at the club to celebrate new ownership and Bob's release from prison. The following weekend on Saturday, the club offered a two for one on beers and half off on top-shelf brands. When Bob showed up, he got a lot of welcomes from the guys he had hired. They were all very happy to see him after so many years. The club was packed as usual, and a girl caught Bob's eye as she walked in. She asked him if he worked here years ago, and he said yes. She told him, "I was the first female server you hired, and after you went away, I did not want to be here anymore." She asked him, "If you're back now, do you have any openings for waitress?"

Bob said, "For you, yes. When can you start?"

She said, "Now if you like?" Bob told her to go to the back and get a shirt and go to work. She came close to him and kissed him on the cheek, thanking him. She then told Bob, "I have a good idea for female patrons. How about something called a girls' night out, where the club is open to only women? You can make it for a Thursday night so it doesn't interfere with the normal business on the weekends."

Bob told her, "Not a bad idea, let me talk to my partner."

She said, "It's just a thought," and went to work. Bob then got with Glenn and told him of the proposal for a Thursday night ladies-only.

Glenn went all in and said, "Let's do it." Glenn then put out the advertising and got the employees together to tell them. He specifically told the bouncers, "There will be no flirting. Stay professional."

They all agreed, and they couldn't wait to see a lot of beautiful women without a guy hanging on them. But they know that they could be worse to deal with than other men. They would attack bouncers by kicking them in the balls, scratching their face and eyes with their nails, and you couldn't really be rough with them.

It was now Thursday night, and the women were starting to come in, some alone and others in groups. The bar and servers were busy but not much with the food; that was a guy thing. The house bands were playing, and the dance floor was packed with the girls screaming and singing to the band's songs.

The ladies' room was also very busy, so Glenn made the men's room into a ladies' room to handle the overflow. He posted a male bouncer at the entrance, making sure no men went inside; the male employees would use a men's room backstage if need be.

Then a female came out of the ladies' room and told the female bouncer at the front door that she should go in and check out the stall, as there were two girls in it. The female bouncer went in and went into the stall next to the one that had two girls in it and stood on the toilet and looked over the divider and saw the girls doing lines of cocaine. She yelled down to them, and they panicked. They quickly tried to hide the coke and then come out. They were told to leave, or the police would be called. The two left without incident.

Now it was getting to that witching hour when everyone has had too much to drink. Several women were falling-down drunk and had to be carried out to the front bench and then they had a cab called for them. It was now closing time and last call was made but the club is clearing out pretty well without incident.

But the girls had to be careful leaving, as the local police sat around the club, waiting for drunk drivers. The club's bartenders were aware that if someone seemed to be too drunk, they were not allowed to serve them any more alcohol.

It was now 3:30 a.m. and the club was cleared out and cleaned up, so many of the bouncers and management went to another local club that closed at 6:00 a.m. Glenn and Bob were very good friends with the management of this other club and were never charged for anything. Then a scuffle broke out between a few of The Hurt's bouncers and the bouncers from this club. Bob saw it and quickly steps in to stop it. He told his guys to knock it off and go have a beer. Bob then talked to the other bouncers and calmed the situation.

He was told that his employees were talking trash about their club and it got a little heated. Bob apologized for his guys and, after a short time, went home. It was a good thing he left because just after he thought he calmed things down, they flared up again but this time worse. As Bob got into his home, he got a call from one of his employees to come back to the club. Bob asked what the problem was, and he was told, "Just after you left, there was a big fight between us and them, and one of them was stabbed." The cops were on scene and the paramedics tending to the stabbing victim. At least this time, Bob was not involved, as he was on probation. Bob arrived back at the club and saw numerous police cars and crime scene tape up around the scene.

Bob approached one of the cops and told him, "I understand some of my employees from my club were involved." The cop told Bob he did not know, but then Bob was met by one of his female servers from his club. Bob asked her, "What the hell happened? I thought things were calmed down after I spoke to everyone."

She told him, "Some of our guys got in the face of one of theirs, and then it was a free for all. And after it finally broke up, one of the other bouncers was bleeding badly from a stab wound to his chest. The knife used was on the ground, and one of our guys was being detained by their management as the culprit. Up the police coming in, they took custody of our guy, who also had blood on his shirt."

Bob then asked, "Where is he?" and she pointed to a police car with his bouncer in the back seat. Bob approached the car with an officer standing next to it. Bob asked the cop if he could speak to his employee, and the officer agreed, telling him to make it fast. Bob leaned over to the window and said, "What the fuck? Didn't I just leave, telling everyone to knock it off? OK, I will get you a lawyer, so don't talk to anyone, got it?"

"Yes."

The stabbing victim was taken to the emergency room and immediately went into surgery. After approximately six hours, the doctors advised that he would be OK after a short hospital stay. The guy's parents were also at the hospital after a long ride from where they lived.

Meanwhile, the guy who did the stabbing, named Mike, was in custody, awaiting a bail hearing on aggravated battery. Mike's attorney said that the other guy would survive and was in the hospital, but Mike said, "I did not do this." He told his lawyer, "We were fighting, and I saw a shiny object out of the corner of my eye. Not knowing what it was, I still fought, and when it was broken up, people were pointing to me. I had blood on me because I was close to him. I never touched a knife or had a knife."

The attorney told Mike that once the DNA was checked, it should help. Mike was given a bail of $25,000. The attorney posted the bail, and Mike was released. A few days later, the DNA only showed the victim's. This was discouraging but not the end of the road.

Then a few days later, the attorney got a call from Bob that someone came forward with a cell phone video of the fight, and guess what it actually showed? It proved that Mike did not stab anyone; in fact, it showed an employee of that club doing the stabbing. This information was brought to the state attorney and then to the judge. After the video was authenticated, the State had no choice but to drop the charges and return the bail money. Mike was very happy and relieved and even went to see the victim at the hospital to tell him that he was sorry. Mike was glad to see the victim getting better.

Bob was glad to see his guy not being the one that committed the crime and welcomed him back to work. Bob told his entire staff to stay clear of the other club for a while until things settled down; they didn't want any problems here with some type of retaliation.

The club had been getting a lot of interest from a movie production company as they were looking for a venue for their film about violence and rock and roll. They had heard many great things about the club because of its layout and size. They asked Bob if they could send out some location scouts to look at the club, and of course, Bob said sure. Bob then got with Glenn and told him about the possible proposal. Glenn said, "Great, let's show them a good time and safe time."

Bob and Glenn got with the staff before opening and told them, "Several movie scouts are coming in this weekend to check out the club for a possible movie shoot. We want everyone to be in proper uniform and professional when they are here. If we are selected, I will request that they use most of our staff, but you know they will also want professional actors. If we are selected, the club will be shut down for a while for filming, and for those who don't get chosen to work on the film, I will still pay your salary." Bob said, "I have a feeling Depp had something to do with this."

It was now the weekend and Saturday and the film crew would be arriving. It was now 10:00 p.m., and a man and woman came in, asking for Bob. One of the staff got Bob from the office and told him that those film people were here.

Bob went up from the office and greeted them and welcomed them to The Hurt. Bob started to show them around the club and backstage. Bob had a cleaning crew come in prior and made sure the place was clean. The film crew took many pictures and many measurements as well as checking out the special lighting and sound system. They also checked the parking lot and exterior of the building. Bob was told that the club sign would have to come down and be replaced with the club's name for the film and maybe a few changes for the inside. Bob said, "Whatever you think is fine."

They told Bob, "We feel this is perfect for our film, but we don't have the last say so. We send all our information to the director and producer, and they decide from other venues, but since Johnny put in a good word, we think that would help." They thanked Bob and departed.

Bob then called Glenn and told him, "They were very impressed, and we will hopefully hear back in a few weeks." A few weeks went by, and Bob got the call he has been waiting for; the club had been chosen for the film shoot. Bob was told that the film crew and actors would start coming in in a few weeks. Bob asked about using some of his staff, as they were experienced and well mannered. He was told, "We hoped that we could use your entire staff along with our actors that will have most of the speaking parts." Bob said, "Great, I will tell the staff." Bob then got the staff together and told them, "The producer of the movie wants to use all of us alongside their actors." The staff yelled out, "Wow, great!" Bob told them that all he expected was for everyone to be professional and patient when dealing with the actors as sometimes there are many versions and takes before the director is happy.

A few days later, Bob got a call from the producer of the film, who now told him what the film was about. He told Bob, "Remember many years ago, there was a fatal shooting of a bouncer here? Well, one of your bouncers from back then wrote a book based on the shooting and the aftermath. Well, we got the script, and it sat on the shelf for years until it was brought to my attention. After reading the script, I felt this would make a great film and may spin off to a series on TV."

Bob said, "Yes, I remember that as I was working that night at the club." Bob told the producer, "We are looking forward to the start." The producer told Bob he will see him soon at the club. A few days went by, and the movie logistics started to arrive: lighting, changing out the club sign outside, a lot of wiring, cameras inside and out.

The director and second unit director arrived mid-day and saw Bob and told him, "We will be working here for the next few days, setting up." Some of the actors also arrived to look around and get a feel of the place, and they liked it very much. The local police also arrived for set security and to shut down the roads around the club. The police and their chief were told, "During the night shoot scenes, there will be gunshots as part of the scenes, and we just want you and your people to be aware." The casting director then told Bob, "Have your staff here tomorrow around noontime so we can get them situated and tell them what they will be doing." Several motor homes were on the club property for the main actors, as well as mobile bathrooms, mobile kitchen, makeup and wardrobe trailer.

The next day, the staff showed up and met with the casting director. The staff was taken to the wardrobe trailer and given their outfits to wear. The girls were given very short shorts and halter tops, and the guys were given jeans and uniform T-shirts. They were then told to go into the club for their positions. They met with the director and were given instructions on what to do and where to be. They met the actors, who seemed very nice. Bob and Glenn were not in the film but would get screen credits. After everyone was in their place, it was rehearsal time. The scene was set, the lights were dimmed, and music was playing. Then you heard, "Action," and everyone moved to where they were directed to go. Bob and Glenn were proud to see their staff do so well. After five takes, the director was happy and it was getting late, so all were released and told to be back at nine in the morning.

The next morning, everyone showed up on time, and security was tight because of an A-list actor that was there as the main character. The police had the filming area shut down; traffic was rerouted away from the club. The hair and makeup trailers were busy, as well as the wardrobe trailer. The food trailer was making breakfast for everyone, and whatever you wanted, they made for you. Then the director asked for the club staff to come into to the club and take their places. The star then came in and took his place. The director yelled out, "Music, lights, and action!" The club staff moved around to their predetermined spots throughout the club, as did the star. The director then yelled, "Cut!"

He then got with one of the staff and told her, "You need to stay in the predetermined area, because you're blocking a shot. Then everybody, places, and action." The scene went well, and the director yelled, "Cut! Great, guys, set up the next shot." While this was going on, the star went to his trailer and waited for his next scene. The director told his assistant to get the star for the next shot, and he did. Inside, all were in place as the star came in. Then one of the staff was overheard saying, "It's good to be king."

The director now wanted to film the ending. The scene was set for the drive-by shooting death of one of the bouncers. Two staff members were in their car, which was parked at the front of the club and others meandering in the parking lot in front.

The director yelled, "Action!" and the car started to back up from the front, when one of them in the car said, "Stop, a car is coming." A station wagon was coming through the lot as the car with the staff stopped. Then as the station wagon drove by, numerous shots rang out into the crowd. The car windows were shattered as one of them yelled, "They are shooting! Get down."

A witness saw a rifle barrel sticking out from the passenger-side window. The car then peeled out of the lot off camera. People were yelling and lying on the ground. All were getting up except for one. The star, who just came out from the club after hearing the shots, ran over to a bouncer lying on the ground, bleeding and moaning. He pulled the bouncer up into his lap as he sat on the ground and put a finger into the bullet hole in an attempt to stop the bleeding.

The star yelled out, "Call 911, call 911!" Then moments later, the paramedics arrived and took the bouncer from the arms of the star. The director then yells cut, great, everyone, let's clean up and set up the next scene." The director said that he would have the special effects folks plug in the gunshot sounds later and darken the outside—film magic. Bob and Glenn were watching the filming and had flashbacks to the true event so many years earlier.

The director then decided to break for the day and resume in the morning. He let everyone know, "Back tomorrow at 8:00 a.m." All the staff agreed and departed for the night. The star went to his hotel on the beach. The next morning, everyone showed up, expecting the star of the film.

CHAPTER 7

The assistant director went to the hotel room and discovered the star missing. He immediately called the director and told him that the star of the film was not at the hotel. The police were notified and responded to the hotel along with some detectives. They searched the hotel room and discovered his wallet and jewelry still there in a drawer. There was no sign of foul play. The detective checked the hotel surveillance cameras and saw that he got to his room approximately 9:00 p.m. the night prior. Then around 11:00 p.m., two women showed up and went inside the room. About 2:00 a.m., he left the room with the women. Then they were seen walking out of the hotel and then out of sight of any cameras.

There was no disturbance in the room, and it appeared that they were laughing as they left the hotel. Further investigation showed him at the hotel bar, where two women met him around 8:00 p.m. the night prior. They sat together for a while before he left alone. Since this was a very high-profile celebrity, the FBI were called in to assist the police with this case. Since the feds and local police were working on finding the star, it was decided to continue to shoot around the scenes involving the star until more information was obtained. The production company in Los Angeles was also notified; they advised they would monitor the case. The filming continued until the FBI came to the set and spoke privately with the director.

The director was told, "We have some bad news. A body was found on the beach in Fort Lauderdale that is believed to be your film star."

The director fell back into his chair and put his head in his hands, asking what happened. The FBI said they did not know yet, but we would like you to come down and look to be sure. The director said of course. The director told his assistant director to finish the scenes for the day and that he would be back later. The director got in the car with the FBI and was escorted to where the body was. The body was located on a rock formation near the shoreline, still in the clothes from the earlier day. The director looked and confirmed that it was his star of the film.

There were no apparent, visible injuries, so the autopsy would confirm a cause of death. The director was beyond words and in shock. He now had to tell the rest of the crew and staff. He then called the production company and told them about the death, and they ordered the film shut down. The director was driven back to the club and then gathered everyone and broke the sad news. Everyone was in disbelief and crying. He then said that the production was shut down by the production company. He thanked everyone for all their work and yelled in a cracking voice, "This is a wrap!" He got with Bob and Glenn and told them that the club would be turned back over to them once they put things back the way they were before the shoot.

They told the director how sorry they were about this tragic time and thanked him for the opportunity. The club was put back together and cleaned up. All the trailers were removed and the club sign put back up. The staff was paid for their time and was sorry to see the film stop. The FBI was working the case along with the homicide unit from Fort Lauderdale PD. During the investigation, the video from the bar was enhanced for facial recognition, and you got a good shot of the two women at the bar.

The pictures were very clear; the FBI lab did a great job enhancing the pictures. The pictures were given to the local news outlets and shown on the TV newscasts.

While Glenn was in his office at the club, he was watching the news, and when the pictures were shown, he fell out of his chair. The two women shown were two of his servers from the club. He immediately notified the FBI and they responded that night to see Glenn. Glenn told them that the women in the pictures worked as servers and that the night in question they left a little early as they were not in any more scenes. The FBI asked if they were working tonight and was told yes, they were scheduled and that should be here by 8:00 p.m. The FBI waited in the club's office as Glenn notified Bob to come to the club ASAP. The time was now 8:45 p.m., and the women were a no-show.

Glenn called them and there was no answer. The FBI asked for and got the addresses for the women. The FBI went to the address of the two women and discovered that they were not home, and it appeared that they had moved out in a hurry. Some clothes were left behind, food, and even a parakeet. They had a car and the FBI was working on finding the vehicle information so it could be put in the system as a BOLO (be on the lookout). At this time, they were persons of interest in the death of the film star. The FBI put out information if they were located, to just detain and call the FBI and not ask any questions of them. While this was going on, the body was autopsied and released to the funeral home so it could be flown back to Los Angeles, California, for burial.

The media was all over this report and staked out the club for interviews as well as them watching the home of the two women. Then the FBI met with Glenn and Bob about the two women and if they ever saw anything that made them look suspicious. Both told the FBI that they did not see anything out of the ordinary and nothing even came up on the background check. The FBI then asked, "Who did the background checks?"

They were told, "A private investigation agency did them, and we will you give you their name." Unfortunately, this was bad press for the club again. The club was mentioned in several local newspapers with a headline to the effect of "local rock club hires criminals." This made Bob very angry, and he called the paper's editor to complain and for them to make a retraction.

The paper revamped their story title, which made Bob feel a little better. The FBI then told Glenn and Bob that they were also investigating similar cases in northern Florida, and the two women fit the description. The only difference was that in those cases, the men did not die; they were only victims of grand theft, reminiscent of the Rolex robbers. At this time, the only evidence they had against the women was that they were the last ones seen with the victim. So until they were found, they would hope to get a confession.

Back in LA, California, the media was going wild to cover the funeral, but of course, during the coverage, they badmouthed Florida and the club. The west coast media reported that the club knowingly hired these women with a criminal background, when in fact there was no criminal history discovered. Then they bashed South Florida for who lives there. But luckily, this bad press did nothing negative toward the club; if anything, more people came in, probably being a little curious, and the others were great repeat patrons. Then Bob had an idea that they would take up a collection for the film star and the club would match it. It would just be a symbolic gesture for how they all felt. After a short time, the patrons and club donated over $10,000 to the family. The staff were upset not only about two of their coworkers possibly being involved in the death but also with the cancellation of the film that would have put The Hurt on the club map.

Bob thought back to when he worked in the club many years earlier and all the deaths attributed to the club: Laura died of cancer, Richie committed suicide, Josh was killed after retirement via a car crash, Randy died of an unknown illness, Jeff (after being accidentally shot during a hunting accident) died of a heart attack and he was also a stuntman in the movies. There was a lot of sadness attached to the club and now this incident involving two female servers. Bob thought when it would end, and even after being set up and going to prison for five years, his fiancée cheating on him with the co-owner, who gets killed by his jealous wife whom he was cheating on. This sounded like a typical soap opera. But with all the heartache came good things. The club was doing well fiscally, the employees were happy, the city was happy as there were minimal complaints and the cops were friendly toward the staff.

A few days later, the FBI contacted Bob at the club and told him that there was a possible sighting of the two women in the Atlanta area and that the Atlanta PD were working a case very similar to the South Florida case. It was possible that the two were working their way north, so now the US Marshall service had the case, and they always prevailed in capturing their prey. The City of Atlanta had many fancy nightclubs, which was good for the two fugitives. The police had put undercovers in each one with the description, and maybe they would get lucky in a capture. After a few weekends, there was no luck; the two did not show up at any Atlanta club. But then a few days later, the marshals got a phone tip that two women fitting the description were eating in a restaurant and their car was parked outside.

The marshals set up and surveyed the restaurant and saw the suspect car outside. They didn't want to make a move in the restaurant, so they waited for them to exit. As they came out, one of the women spotted a cop and made a run to the car and quickly got in, leaving her friend outside. She could not leave because the car was blocked in, so she panicked and pulled a gun and told her friend that she was sorry and shot her through the window then turned the gun on herself, and with a shot to the head, she killed herself. This was an unfortunate end to a murder investigation.

The scene was secured for the crime scene unit. The local media was also now on scene, and it became a breaking news story. The FBI was notified of the outcome, and in turn, they notified Bob and Glenn at the club, who were sorry to hear the news but glad it was over and no one else would be hurt.

When the crime scene detective checked the car, they found the SAG (Screen Actors Guild) card belonging to the movie star, proving they were with him. The suspects' car was removed, and the scene cleaned up. The medical examiner responded to remove the bodies for an autopsy. The movie star's family was also notified by the FBI, and they were grateful that they and the marshals were ok. Word then spread pretty quickly throughout the South Florida club community. Ironically, Hollywood filmmakers wanted to do a film on the case and how it played out. Bob was deluged with calls from movie producers wanting information on the two women and wanting to bring their film to South Florida and actually film in the club where they worked.

It was like déjà vu, a film company wanting to use the club for the story and to use the staff but bring in two actresses to play the parts of the two women suspects. Bob was elated again and told Glenn, who also felt the same way. Weeks went by, and Bob got the contracts and permits needed and got a start date for a few more weeks. After a few weeks, Bob met with the director and producer at the club, and they said, "We love what we see. We will not make any changes to the club, and we will use the same."

Bob told them he would get with the police department for security and traffic control. They said, "Great, let's make a movie." The next day, the FBI came in and completed background checks on everyone involved with the film and the club owners. The day of the shoot, the main star had a personal bodyguard that stayed very close at all times. This film crew was very approachable by the club staff and very helpful during the filming. Each day, the filming took between ten and fourteen hours. The filming went very smoothly with very few takes, and the staff was excellent also. The film was completed in approximately two months and then taken to LA production for editing and sound.

After the filming, there was a wrap party, which everyone attended. The director gathered everyone and gave a special thanks to all involved and took up a collection for the fallen star that was murdered. At the end of the party, the crew started to dismantle the set and gather up all the gear. The trailers were removed, and the club returned to normal. The following weekend, Bob and Glenn had bragging rights when it came to advertising the club, stating the famous Hurt rock-and-roll club now featured in a new film. Well, this brought in a new amount of clientele, and for many months, the club was always packed, making everyone who worked there a lot of money.

Bob and Glenn then kept up ladies' night and many other specials throughout the year. While in the club's office, Bob had a call from the local newspaper, which wanted to interview him about the two women he hired that turned out to be murderers. He said sure and brought Glenn into the fray. The next day, well before the club opened, they met with a reporter and photographer. The reporter introduced himself along with the photographer. Bob was a little skeptical of reporters as he did not get a fair shake when he was set up and jailed.

The first question from the reporter was "How can you hire two murderers?" Bob and Glenn were stunned by that question. Glenn chimed in and said, "You just blew the interview" and asked him to leave. They had a feeling this was a setup but went with it anyway to see where it went. The reporter said it was a fair question and was now told by Bob to get out, so the reporter and photographer left the club, and on the way out, the photographer turned to the reporter and called him an asshole.

Glenn was now back with the sheriff's office, working his shift, and he got called down to the sheriff's headquarters and met with the sheriff along with internal affairs. Glenn was a little surprised, not knowing what was happening. The sheriff asked Glenn if he was part owner of a club and Glenn said yes. He was then asked if he had written permission from the agency, and he said, "No, I did not know I needed it."

The internal affairs detective then asked, "Is there a liquor license under your name?" and Glenn responded yes.

"Again, did you have written permission for that?" And Glenn responded again that he did not know he needed it. The sheriff advised Glenn, "In fact, you did need to get permission, and until our investigation is concluded, you are suspended with pay. Please turn over your badge and ID card to the detective."

Glenn told the sheriff that he should have been afforded his PBA rep and not have been ambushed this way. Glenn was then dismissed and he left. He then got with Bob and told him the story, and Bob felt bad about it but could not do anything.

Since Glenn was now suspended, he spent more time at the club, and as many days and months went by, Glenn got more depressed as he missed his job. He then got a letter from the sheriff telling him that his status was changed to without pay. Now he was out of work, with no real income, although he was getting a small check from the club. He told Bob that he was falling behind on bills as well as his health fading from stress.

Then one night at the club, he was introduced to a guy who turned out to be a big crack cocaine dealer with a lot of connections and protection. Glenn was given an opportunity to make a lot of money in a short amount of time. All he had to do was drive this crack dealer around a few times per week and he could make a couple of grand cash.

Glenn told this guy he would think about it because he could not get caught, as he hoped to get back on the sheriff's office.

A few days later, Glenn called this guy and told him he would do it as long as he did not carry a weapon and get involved in any violence. The crack dealer said, "Sure, no sweat. You cannot tell anyone what you're doing."

Glenn said, "I got it."

"OK, then, meet up this Monday around 9:00 p.m. at the 7-Eleven and we will go from there."

Glenn started driving this guy around as he collected money and distributed his product. Glenn was very petrified about getting caught and that not only losing his job but going to prison.

Well, this went on for a few months without a hitch, and Glenn was making good money but still missed his job. Glenn did not know that the sheriff's narcotics unit was working with DEA, who got a tip on this crack dealer. During one of Glenn's runs with the dealer, his car was pulled over by the sheriff's office and followed by the DEA. A felony stop was conducted on the car, and both Glenn and the dealer were removed from the car without incident. The streets surrounding the stop were shut down as the two were handcuffed. Then the on-duty sergeant drove up and saw Glenn lying on the ground, handcuffed. Glenn looked up at the sergeant and said, "Sarge, I didn't do anything."

The sergeant then said, "So why are you on the ground in cuffs?" The sergeant had no idea that his guy was involved with the biggest crack dealer in the area, and he knew that Glenn was on suspension; now he would probably be fired and jailed. The two suspects are put in a patrol car and taken to the office for interviews. Both lawyered up, so they were booked on narcotics charges and taken to jail. The sergeant told Glenn, "I'm very disappointed, as you had a shot at coming back to the road, but you really fucked that up, didn't you?"

One of the deputies that knew Bob from the club called him and told him about Glenn's arrest, and Bob was furious. His liquor license was at stake. Now Bob would have to find someone else to get the license, as he can't because he too is a convicted felon. The next day, in bond court, Glenn was able to bond out with the help of some family.

Glenn contacted Bob, and they met the following day at a coffee shop. Bob told Glenn, "You have to sell your part of the club, and I will buy it from you for what you paid and I'm sorry we have to part ways now. I cannot be around you since part of my probation is that I cannot be around other felons. So I will have someone bring your personal items from the club to your home, and damn it, you really fucked up, man, the driver for the biggest crack dealer in the county, with the DEA involved, wow. Well, good luck and I hope they give you a break because if you go to prison, you will be segregated from the others because you're an ex-cop." After a few months, the trials started, and the crack dealer got fifteen years and Glenn eight years since it was his first offense—a sad ending to a pretty good career.

After about fifteen months, Glenn was escorted by a guard to the library and viciously attacked by two guys who beat him very badly as the guard looked the other way. Glenn was beaten so badly that he had to be in the hospital for three months while they fixed his broken bones and stab wounds. He was told that he would never have his own kids and full use of his arms—they were so broken up. He needed new teeth as the fronts were kicked out; he was better off dead. After his hospital stay, he was transferred to another facility, which was more secure. The investigation by the federal corrections revealed that the crack dealer felt that Glenn turned on him and that he needed to be dealt with. So the dealer was able to get money to a few other inmates to have them commit this attack.

The corrections department charged the dealer with attempted murder as to the other inmates involved. After a short trial, all were given a life term. Because of Glenn's injuries, the department of corrections released him early to a rehab center; he was never the same, and it was a fall from grace. Was this another black eye for the club? Bob was beside himself and now had to search for a new partner to keep the liquor license. But then out of nowhere, Bob got a call from LA, and it was a partner of Johnny Depp that heard about the club's problem and wanted to help. He made Bob an offer as a silent partner and liquor license applicant to save the club. Without that license, the club could only sell beer, and the money was in the liquor sales.

This proposal to Bob was accepted, and the silent partner was able to obtain the license to sell liquor. Bob was happy because this guy had connections with famous powerful people that the club could prosper from, but did Bob make the right move? Was Bob just happy to get a guy in that could get the liquor license, without really knowing him? Bob and his attorney sent this guy the paperwork to sign and get half of the club. Bob was a little standoffish with this guy as he kept throwing Depp's name around, but Bob did not want to call Johnny and bother him. The paperwork was sent and signed, giving half ownership away and the liquor license. The guy from LA called Bob and told him he would be coming into town and would see him and the club.

The following week, this guy showed up along with two no necks looking like mobsters. They all went to the office, where Bob was told of some changes these guys wanted. Bob looked at the other two and told them that any changes would be discussed between him and the new half owner. The other two then stood up in a threatening manner and looked at Bob in a menacing way until the other owner told them to stay seated, then told them to go out and get a drink. They left, leaving Bob and this guy, now known as Mr. Jones, alone to talk business.

Mr. Jones told Bob that he wanted to bring in a money guy to look over the books and some "special girls" to work in the club. "They will make us a lot of money, believe me."

Bob told him that he ran a legit business and wanted no monkey business and then told him about his felony arrest and conviction. Mr. Jones told Bob, "Don't worry, pal. All will be well." Mr. Jones then said that he wanted a few stripper nights that brought in the bigger money. Bob was not too keen on that idea but felt that strippers do bring in a lot of cash. So Bob agreed and ordered two stripper poles to be installed on the stage. They then decided to have stripper night twice a week, one weeknight and one weekend night. Then Bob was curious to ask about Mr. Jones's relationship with Johnny Depp and confronted him on it.

Mr. Jones told Bob that he was an acquaintance and did some work for him in the past and nothing more. Bob then said, "I thought you were partners with him?"

Mr. Jones basically said, "Not really a partner but a special friend."

Bob said, "I see," and gave a little laugh. Mr. Jones turned away and walked out. Mr. Jones grabbed his two friends and walked toward the front door, when they saw a police car out front. They quickly turned around and went out the back, as they didn't like cops, which will be explained later. They got into their car and departed the club. Bob was now getting a little suspicious about the new part owner, but other than that, no evidence of any wrongdoing.

The following night, Mr. Jones showed back up at the club with his boys and started looking into the books. He sat down with Bob and went through the books and told Bob, "The numbers should be higher than they are, so we have to fix that." Mr. Jones told one of his guys to go to the car and get some of their own spreadsheets. One of the goons took the club's books and transcribed them into their ledger showing a loss for tax purposes, so now they wanted to keep two sets of books, one for the club and one for the IRS.

Bob then jumped up and said, "Hell no, we will keep the correct bookkeeping. I'm not going to jail for tax evasion."

Mr. Jones then told his guys to step out of the office while he talked with Bob, and they did. Mr. Jones told Bob, "This is how it's going to be and if you don't like it, too bad, and if you report it to anyone, it will be too bad for you." Mr. Jones then left the room as Bob stayed behind. He put his head in his hands and sat there for a few minutes. He then got up and went to the bar for a drink.

Mr. Jones and his guys had left the club. Now Bob felt like he was between a rock and a hard place, so he went along. But now Bob felt that he had to protect himself, and he started recording all his conversations with Mr. Jones.

Meanwhile, the club was set up for stripper night, and as time went by, it was very productive for the club. A lot of money was being made, and the servers were also doing well. Bob started to notice a different class of people coming in on stripper nights. At times, it looked like mob night. This was what Bob wanted to avoid and to stay out of trouble and prison. But as time went on, all was well.

The club had no problems and the staff was happy. After a few months, rumors were floating around that the feds were going to be coming down hard on a club in south Florida, but no one knew which club it was. But the club's activities went on without a hitch for many months, and Mr. Jones was a pretty good partner, other than the two sets of books that they were keeping and the mob types that came to the club.

The club was doing very well, and the money was rolling in big time. So Mr. Jones spoke to Bob about opening up another club but this time strictly an adult club. This was where the money was in south Florida. Bob said he would think about it for a few days. Bob thought that he could get a nicer home and car and have better financial security if the adult club came to fruition.

So a few days later, Bob got with Mr. Jones and told him, "Let's do it, let's make the big money." The two then got together and found a building for lease in the downtown Fort Lauderdale area. Mr. Jones would have to get the liquor license since Bob was a convicted felon. They signed the lease and started to build the interior as an upscale adult nightclub. The club would have a big stage for musical acts, stripper poles, a great sound-and-lighting system and very professional armed security. This way the club would entice the high-money people that liked to party.

So of course, this type of club would also entice the criminal enterprise. The club would need a lot of cash to get off the ground, so Bob and Mr. Jones discussed the finances, and Bob was told, "Don't worry. I know people." Bob asked what and who, and he was told, "I got this. Don't worry." So Mr. Jones went out of town for a few days and came back with the funds needed to get the club built. Bob asked where the cash infusion came from, and he was told, "Friends."

Now the club was being built and was coming along under the watchful eye of Mr. Jones, as Bob was busy back at The Hurt. Then believe it or not, Bob got wind of who gave the cash for the new club, and he was astonished. The two guys that he fired from the club many months before were the money men on the new club. And to make it worse, the two men were the sons of the two convicted killers of the bouncer over twenty-five years earlier.

Bob could not believe what he had learned. He then went to Mr. Jones and told him, "No way are we taking money from these assholes. Do you know who they are? These guys' fathers were convicted of killing my friend and fellow bouncer many years ago." Mr. Jones told Bob he knew about them, but they had big money and wanted a part of this new club. Bob told Mr. Jones, "I'm very uncomfortable with these two assholes being involved. I cannot go along with it."

Mr. Jones told Bob, "It is too bad that you don't like these guys, but I do, and you have no choice as partner in this venture." Finally, Bob met these two guys, and when he met them, he was not very pleasant. Right off the bat, Bob told these guys that he wished that their fathers got the electric chair after they killed his friend.

One of these guys told Bob that his dad got raped in prison and contracted AIDS and was let out early so he could go home to die, and he did. Then one of these guys told Bob that if they could get rid of him, they would in a heartbeat. Bob told them to take their best shot and walked away. The two investors now conspire to get rid of Bob as he might be a hindrance to their plans.

Bob was not happy with the antics and criminal acts Mr. Jones might be involved in, so he contacted his lawyer to see about getting out of the contract he signed with Mr. Jones. When Bob met with his attorney a few days later at the law office, he ran into Mr. Jones, who asked Bob why he wanted to get out of the contract.

Bob told Mr. Jones, "I'm not happy with the relationship and where it is heading, plus having to deal with the two scumbags whose parents killed my friend." He then told Bob that if he got out of the contract too soon, he would lose everything that he put into The Hurt.

So now Bob had had enough of Mr. Jones and started to think how he could get him out of his life. Bob decided to take out a huge loan against The Hurt and hire a hit man to kill Mr. Jones and his two henchmen. This was a big move, and he felt it was the only way out and knew that if he got caught, he would go to prison for life. Bob thought about it for a few days and decided to go through with it.

CHAPTER 8

Bob contacted a guy he was in prison with and met him in the parking lot of the club. He told the guy what he wanted done, and if it went through, it would be $10,000 per hit. Bob agreed and gave half up front, $15,000. Bob conspired with his prison friend to get Mr. Jones to the club on a pretext and shoot him. A few days later, Mr. Jones was summoned to The Hurt by Bob and met him outside around 2:00 a.m.; the club was closed. As they talked, a shadowy figure came from behind and fired one round into the back of the head of Mr. Jones. He fell dead to the ground. The suspect ran away, and Bob left the area. The following morning, Bob arrived at the club and first pretended to find Mr. Jones dead and then called 911 to report the murder. The police and paramedics arrived, and the scene was secured for the homicide detectives.

Luckily for Bob, there were no cameras outside, and he was not on his phone the night of the murder. Bob told the detectives that he was home sleeping, and when he arrived at the club, he found Mr. Jones. Bob told the detectives that Mr. Jones was a partner investor in the club. The scene was held by the police for over eight hours until it was released. The blood was cleaned up, and the club stayed closed for one more day. Bob then got in touch with the suspect and told him where the two friends of Mr. Jones would be the following morning very early: "They like a small coffee shop near the tracks, and when they come out, there won't be anyone else around, so you can finish the job and collect the rest of the money." The following night, the two henchmen were gunned down outside the coffee shop as they left.

Again, there were no witnesses just an ear witness and no cameras. The ear witness was the coffee shop waitress who went outside and saw the two bodies then called 911. Upon arrival of the police, the scene was secured until Homicide and crime scene were there. Bob was then notified on his burner phone of the shooting by the suspect, who expected the rest of the payment. Bob said no sweat and met him a few miles away for the rest of the payment. Approximately a week later, Bob went to see his attorney about the cancellation of the contract he had with Mr. Jones. He was successful in ending it now that one half was deceased. Bob then ended his involvement in the new club they were working on as he did not want to deal with the two assholes that were the money men.

Bob now felt vindication and went back to managing the Hurt, which was where he felt more comfortable. But he still needed to find someone to come in and get the liquor license; since Mr. Jones was dead, the license died with him. Bob had an idea that might get him in trouble, but he wanted to give it a shot. He felt that if he changed his name and got a new social security number, he could then apply and hopefully get the liquor license. So he went to the courthouse and filled out the appropriate paperwork to legally change his name, which was now Anthony Grossman. Bob now applied for the liquor license from the State of Florida, but it was flagged by the ABT (Alcoholic Beverage and Tobacco agency).

The address for the license showed two prior owners, and the state agents wanted to know why. So now Anthony has to come up with a good reason he tried to deceive the state about the liquor license. He contacted his lawyer and told him what he did. The lawyer told Anthony, "If you lied on the license form, being a convicted felon could land you back in prison. So did you lie?"

Anthony said, "I do not think so, just that I used my new legal name on the form." The lawyer did not think it was too big a deal, and if the state made something of it, a fine might be in order and nothing else. Then two state investigators came to see Anthony in the club. They went to the office and pulled out the license request form and the other licenses held by the club over the past year.

Most were explained away, but when it came to the new request, the state felt that Anthony was purposely deceiving the state in an attempt to get the liquor license. The investigators felt there was a crime here but decided to confer with the state attorney before any arrest would be made. They told Anthony that it did not look good and that if the state attorney felt there was probable cause for an arrest, they would be back. The investigators then thanked Anthony and departed. Anthony immediately called his lawyer and discussed the meeting. The attorney told Anthony, "If you get called to the state attorney's office, call me, and I will be there too. A few days later, Anthony was summoned to the state attorney's office, and he brought his attorney. They all had a meeting about the liquor license.

The state attorney felt there was not sufficient evidence to support a charge but requested the state to impose a $1,000 fine on Anthony and a clear warning that the shenanigans will cease immediately, or he would face charges. Anthony and his attorney agreed and departed. Anthony then felt like a brick wall was lifted off him, but he still needed to get someone in the club that could legally get a liquor license. The attorney went back to his office as Anthony went back to the club. He did not know anyone that could come in and get the license, so he advertised for a second owner who would be able to get the license. Then Anthony got a call from a corporation that was interested in becoming part owner and could get the license.

This corporation had several different types of legitimate clubs in its portfolio and wanted in on the rock club. Eventually, Anthony met with the corporate heads at a nearby hotel and discussed the partnership and the liquor license. Anthony was up front with the businessmen about everything that went down at the club involving the liquor license, and they said, "No problem, we are used to it. It's the nature of the business." Anthony had a good feeling about his new partners as they had a pretty good background working with clubs. Eventually they got the liquor license issue settled and moved forward. The Hurt was profitable and without any problems. All the employees were happy as well as the house bands and the local police as they were at the club many times for numerous problems.

Then approximately two weeks later, as the cooks were cooking in the kitchen, a fire broke out and at first they did not realize, then it got out of control pretty fast. The cooks felt they could quickly put out the fire, but even with all their efforts, they had no luck. The band was playing, people were dancing on the dance floor, and all were having a good time, not knowing what was about to happen.

One of the kitchen help thought it would be a good idea to put water on a grease fire, and when he did, it flashed up and onto one of the cooks, who quickly caught fire. The cook then ran out of the kitchen and onto the dance floor while on fire. People then panicked and screamed as they tried to put the fire out on the cook. Meanwhile, patrons panicked and ran toward the exits, but they were blocked.

The fire raged on and got bigger as it now spread into the main part of the club. Other patrons ran to the front door, but because numerous patrons attempted to get out at the same time, almost no one got out. Now the fire was out of control along with a lot of dense killer smoke. Anthony was able to fight his way to one of the exits and force open the door, but then fell to the sickening smoke. The fire started to burn itself out, but the smoke was thick and poisonous. The fire department finally arrived and pushed their way into the club only to find dozens of victims dead or dying on the floor. Numerous bodies were removed by the paramedics as the firemen put the fire out and vented the club out.

The police were also on scene along with the fire marshal and homicide detectives now working a mass casualty crime scene. Several paramedics were doing CPR in an attempt to save several of the victims. But as the victims were removed and laid outside on a tarp, there were ninety-five dead and twenty being treated. This was a very tragic event, and questions would come up about the blocked exits and the club's capacity. Anthony was one to survive, and he woke up in the hospital. When the detectives went to see Anthony in the hospital, he had no idea what really happened and how many were dead and injured. He was told how many died, and he almost immediately fell into a deep depression. He started to scream and cry and ask how it happened.

He was told that a fire started in the kitchen and quickly spread, and if the exits were not blocked, many more would have survived. The detectives told Anthony to not say anything until he got a lawyer as this might turn into a criminal investigation due to the number of deaths. Anthony thanked the detectives and they left. The state fire marshal conducted his investigation along with the homicide detectives. The case was presented to the state attorney for review as the fire marshal completed his investigation. The state attorney would not file criminal charges, which was a relief to Anthony and his investors, but the families would file a civil wrongful death lawsuit, which most definitely would be the end of The Hurt club as millions of dollars in lawsuits would come down on Anthony and the other owners for their negligence in not keeping the exits clear of debris.

Anthony knew that these lawsuits would take months to get together, so this gave him time to heal. As the months rolled by, Anthony was served with numerous subpoenas, but the lawyers could not locate the other owners so they could be served. They sent out private investigators to the last known addresses, and these were vacant. The landlord of those apartments was told by the other owners that they would be out of town for a while and to forward their mail to a PO box in town. It appeared that the other owners fled the country in an attempt to avoid any civil court proceedings.

Poor Anthony was left holding the bag. Anthony got a civil attorney to handle the court cases, but he knew that the insurance he had was not enough to cover all the millions the cases would produce.

Anthony went home and he was in a deep depression and he felt that the only way out was going out permanently. A few hours after getting home, a neighbor heard a loud bang like a gunshot and called the police. Upon their arrival they made entry into Anthony's home via an unlocked door and found him on the couch, dead from a gunshot wound. On the night that he was supposed to meet with his attorney, he took his life by a gunshot to the head. When the homicide detectives arrived, they discovered a suicide note stating that he was sorry for all the loss of life and only wanted to run a popular nightclub—a sad ending to a guy who always wanted to own a rock-and-club. It seemed like the curse of The Hurt went on. This made big news and even made the news in LA, California, where Johnny Depp lived. Through a spokesperson, Johnny sent his condolences to Anthony's family and to all those who were killed and injured.

The two other investors were never located to face a trial, but the search continued. Meanwhile, the investigation into the fatal club fire was moving slowly. ATF took the case and, with the help of the federal fire marshal, discovered that the fire was deliberately set. It appeared that some wiring sabotage caused an overload of power and thus the fire. The ATF also felt that the exits were probably blocked by the same person on the night of the fire, which meant that Anthony most likely did nothing wrong and prematurely killed himself. The destroyed kitchen had a security camera, which was partially destroyed but the SIM card was not. It was taken to the FBI crime lab where the video of the deadly night was still intact.

The video showed a tall white male with a baseball cap and dark glasses on, with a large tattoo on the top of his right hand messing with wiring on the wall. The video then showed this person walking out of the kitchen into the main room as the wiring on the wall started to smolder. This was the mass murderer who then slipped out of the club. The ATF questioned many employees and showed them a picture from the video of the white male suspect. One bouncer who was not injured recognized the person with a tattoo on his hand as one of the investors as he was seen in the club with Anthony many times. This was a great lead for the ATF. They turned this information over to the FBI so they could put the suspect on their "ten most wanted" list, and then this was turned over to the US Marshals service.

The investigation revealed that the club was bleeding cash, so the other investors started the fire for a large insurance payout. But not so fast, once this was determined to be criminal homicide, no insurance would be paid out. So now there was an international manhunt on for the two other investors. Many federal agencies were involved in this investigation, which would take them into Europe. The FBI released photos of the two wanted suspects, and a hotline number; they even got it on the TV show *America's Most Wanted*.

Back at The Hurt, the building was roped off with crime scene tape as the investigation continued. Many patrons and employees of the club gathered around for a candlelight vigil for those injured and killed in the fire. There were hundreds in the parking lot along with many media outlets.

During the vigil, reporters were going through the crowd, asking about their thoughts on what had happened. Many felt bad for those who were killed, but many loved Anthony and were saddened that he killed himself when there was no need for him to do that. In a bizarre twist, sightings were called into the tip line that one of the suspects was at the vigil; the FBI received numerous calls as to that. The tips were filtered down to the local law enforcement who were at the vigil. The entire area was sealed off as the police moved in on who they thought was one of the suspects. As others in the crowd were pushed away, numerous officers surrounded this one person, leaving no escape.

They pulled down the hood of the hoodie he was wearing and asked for ID. He did not have any, but he looked like the picture that the police had. They then lifted up his sleeve, and there it was, the infamous tattoo. This was one of the suspects who never actually left the area. He was handcuffed and immediately taken from the scene to the police station, where he was met by FBI agents and homicide detectives from the PD. He told the investigators that he never left with his friend because he felt horrible about what had happened and that sooner or later, I would be caught. After hours of interrogation, he confessed to messing with the wires that purposely caused the fire for insurance reasons. The FBI did not investigate homicide as that is a state crime but they do investigate civil rights violations. This suspect felt that he would get the death penalty, so after speaking with his lawyer, he decided to not go to trial and take a plea of guilty to first degree murder. The families were OK with it so they would not have to sit through a lengthy trial. The judge gave him life without parole, and he was immediately taken to prison. Meanwhile, the search continued for the second suspect.

The fire investigation was now complete, and the findings were that someone tampered with the wiring in the club's kitchen which caused the fire and ultimate deaths. This was mostly already known by law enforcement. But now, many of the past employees wanted to rebuild the club as there was not much fire damage but a lot of smoke damage. They were able to get friends to help, and several of the home building stores to donate many items such as wood, flooring, lighting, and many other things. As they started to rebuild, the building leasing company forgave one year of lease payments to help out. So this rebuild continued for approximately four months until completion. The club was now better than before and would have a grand opening soon.

The opening night included many employees from another rock club, city officials, and local celebrities. The anonymous new owners had a grand reopening and dedicated it to the original owner Anthony Grossman, who tragically and needlessly took his life. The local police stood guard over the parking lot and large crowds as well as the local streets for any traffic problems. The opening was terrific—free drinks and food, and raffles for free stuff to support those families who were impacted by the deadly fire. Many of their families were in attendance, and they thanked the owners for inviting them. But as things went, many of the attendees got very ill days later, after the closing of the first night.

The local hospitals were filling up with very sick people with high fevers, shortness of breath, and coughing. This was an unknown illness to the many doctors that were treating the sick. Weeks later, many had died, which led to an investigation by the CDC (Centers for Disease Control). The possible virus was traced back to the club, so inspectors from the CDC came into the club, wearing body suits and breathing protection. They took swabs from everything and then from the employees. A few days later, it was revealed that the virus was all over the club, and many of the employees were infected but showed no symptoms. Some days later, several of the employees were taken to the hospital with breathing problems.

They were immediately put on a ventilator to help them breathe, and they had their blood checked. Several of the employees succumbed to the virus, which now had many frightened and thinking if they were next. The club owners had the club cleaned from top to bottom, and then when the health inspectors came back, the club got a clean bill of health with some exceptions to opening back up. Anyone coming in had to have their temperature taken, and all had to have a mask. So now, the club reopened with those measures in place, which no one had a problem with. But most were still skeptical about coming into the club, so it was slow to being filled up and profitable. Over the next few months, the anxiety wore off and the club started to fill up and profits were good.

The news was hard to watch as they kept on reporting how many people had died from this invisible threat and how many were testing positive. But mixed messages were coming from Washington, DC. But they got through it and moved on and stopped watching the news, as it was depressing. Things were going great for a while, then one day on the news, other police were involved in killing a suspect. A white police officer had killed a black suspect in a nearby city, and it was all caught on cell phone video. As clear as day, an officer had his knee on the neck of the suspect, and all you heard was "I can't breathe." Bystanders were yelling that the suspect could not breathe.

But the police did nothing except keep pressure on the neck as others did nothing. Then the potentially lifeless body of the suspect was put on a gurney by the arriving paramedics and taken to the hospital where he was pronounced dead. Well, the world went crazy. Almost immediately the civil disturbances started, and it was time to hate the police. Black Lives Matter reared its ugly head, making threats to kill the police, and soon thereafter, the riots and looting started, happily joined by the terror group antifa and other anarchists bent on destruction and murder.

Almost immediately, many protests showed up in many big cities around the country. New York City, Minneapolis, Seattle, Portland, and many others erupted with much violence, much turned at the police. Eventually the National Guard was called in to back up the police at the massive violent protests. Hundreds of stores and buildings were destroyed, looted, as well as innocent civilians being attacked, and some killed. The police suffered many injuries and several fatalities from the "peaceful" protesters.

Then the infamous slogan spread with the help of the media and Democrats, "defund the police." Black Lives Matter became so popular with the protesters that the mayor of DC let it be painted on the street leading to the White House. The lamestream media loved it, as did many Democrats in Congress. Throughout the country, there are many thousands that took to the streets chanting "defund the police" and "abolish the police," but many believed that this would get Trump reelected.

And during these "peaceful" protests, many hundreds of police officers were assaulted and killed as well as civilians, along with many millions of dollars in damage to businesses and from looting. Many of the democratic city and state leaders felt that the protests were healthy and long in coming because of systematic racism. People in Congress, some police and military on the street, and entertainers took a knee in support of Black Lives Matter. It was funny that all those attacking the government had no problem taking the benefits from the same government. There were many companies providing shirts stating Black Lives Matter, along with buttons, as if no other lives mattered, and the idiotic companies were coming down on law enforcement and had no problem with what the terror group stands for. "The only good cop is a dead cop," "pigs in a blanket, fry 'em like bacon," how soon they forget.

But now the club owners were fearful of staying open as possible protesters might get drunk and cause trouble and cause damage. The club owners hired a private security team for external protection, which included several K-9s. The club owners told all their employees that nothing other than the club uniform shirts would be worn while on or off duty in the club, and if anyone was caught wearing something else, they would be terminated.

The club did have several black employees, but they seemed pretty cool with everything that was going on. The police notified the club owners that there might be a small protest near the club and to be on the lookout. Then the black male employees did the unthinkable. They had a knock at the rear door of the club, and standing there was a black male asking for food. When the door was opened, the black male rushed in, followed by about a dozen others that burst into the kitchen, then into the main room. They started to throw bottles, knock over tables, and start fights. But luckily, they were outmatched by the many large bouncers who kicked the intruders' asses. All were detained until the police were summoned.

The two kitchen employees were immediately terminated and charged by the police as well. It was later learned that the two kitchen employees were being recruited by the BLM people. Then one night, the managers were walking by the front door and overheard several white bouncers talking about antifa as if they were the greatest things on the planet. They also heard them talk bad about the cops. Well, this did not sit well with the managers, and they then confronted the bouncers about what they heard. The managers immediately fired those bouncers that thought antifa was great and the cops were bad. The managers did not share their opinion as they had law enforcement in their families and they felt that the antifa were a terror organization and they did not want them in the club.

The bouncers felt that it was not right for them to be fired and told the managers that they would be sorry. They then departed the club without incident. The managers felt this was a terroristic threat made toward them and called the police. When the police arrived, the bouncers were already gone. The police got their addresses to follow up. The police went to the homes of the fired bouncers, and when they arrived, the police were not let into the homes. The bouncers told the police, "Get off the property, and with no warrant, you need to leave." The police felt this to be a little odd as they just wanted to talk with them. So the police left and met with the detectives, who did a background check, which did not reveal much.

But then the detectives did a federal check via homeland security and discovered that the two bouncers were on the do-not-fly list because of terroristic threats made on an airplane, against the pilot. They were never arrested but spoken to by the FBI and then put on the no-fly list. The detectives then felt that the two bouncers needed to be watched and felt that something might just happen to the club managers or to the club. Approximately two days later, one of the bouncers was followed to a gun store, where he purchased several handguns and ammo. There was a waiting period of three days before the guns could be picked up. After the third day, the bouncer was seen picking up the guns and then meeting with a suspicious person a few streets away. It appeared that the guns were seen being handed off to this person, so the detectives were able to get the tag number of that car and follow the car. The car was followed to an abandoned warehouse where several other cars were parked.

The detectives ran the tag of the suspect's car and came back to a w/m in a nearby city. This person did not have a criminal history. So the detective ran the other car tags, which revealed several registered owners with a felony conviction. Several of the charges involved shootings and threats. So if they were in possession of the guns, it was a felony. The detectives quickly called up the SWAT commander and told him of the situation, so the SWAT commander called up the team. The SWAT team met with the detectives within thirty minutes, and they were briefed and that guns were involved. The team suited up and came up with a quick plan to get entry as the detectives stayed outside.

Since they did not have a search warrant, they had to go in on exigent circumstances. The team set up and approached an open window and threw in several flash-bangs; they then burst in, taking all into custody without incident. They then called in the detectives and found a stash of weapons, homemade bombs, gasoline, and knives as well as the two bouncers fired from the club. And hanging on the wall was an antifa flag. The detective thought they really hit the jackpot. A check of the guns showed many were reported stolen in burglaries from several homes. The detectives called for more marked units to transport the suspects and collected all the weapons discovered.

The detectives then called the FBI, who came in and took the case as a homeland security case. When the feds take the case, the punishments are more serious than the state's charges. The FBI was very grateful for all the work the detectives and SWAT did and made sure their chief knew. Since the president and Congress made the antifa a terror organization, the members were charged under the terrorism statute and kept in jail without bond. The FBI investigation was widespread, and it showed that there were several clubs that were recruiting new members to strengthen the organization. The group had their eyes on The Hurt club since it had many young impressionable people.

There was a deal in the works to sell the club to a small group of young investors for a lot of money. It was a hard deal to pass up, and the owners did not pass on it and did sell the club for an undisclosed amount. A few weeks later, the sale was final, and the new owners took over and fired the entire staff to bring their own people in. The staff was not very happy as they stayed with the club throughout all its previous problems. The new staff looked very unsavory. The staff was known to carry weapons on the property, and they took no shit from anyone. It looked like a group of thugs just got released from prison—long hair and many tattoos.

The management changed many of the club's rules: the staff could drink on duty, wear whatever they wanted, make out with their girlfriends, and even take a break to have sex in the back room. The good name of The Hurt was now tarnished. Many of the club's employees caught the eyes of the FBI because of their suspicious backgrounds. But the FBI could not make a move on them yet, as the evidence they needed was not there. One night, a moving van came to the back door of the club and offloaded many AR-15 rifles and boxes of ammo. They also had many bulletproof vests and flash-bangs, the same ones the SWAT teams use. One of the club's employees was an FBI informant, and no one knew it, luckily. He then notified the FBI, who then contacted the ATF.

Based on the informant's information and eyewitness testimony, the FBI got a search warrant and arrest warrant for the club's owner. Much later in the evening, when the club was open, the raid was commenced by the FBI and ATF SWAT teams with the assistance of the local police. The raid went off without a hitch. The guns were recovered and the club owner arrested. The club owner was also a convicted felon, which was another felony. All the guns were stolen from a gun store along with the ammo. The next day, the informant was placed in the witness protection program because of the seriousness of the incident.

The club owner agreed to give a statement in exchange for a lesser charge. The feds and US attorney agreed. The club owner told the feds that he and several others were planning a mass killing of the Black Lives Matter group as they felt that organization was a terror group. The mass killing was to take place in a week at a planned protest. The club was to be used as a front for the others in the group to gather. The club owner agreed to a five-year prison term due to his cooperation. Because of his statement, several others working in the club were arrested on federal charges of terrorism. The feds also recovered numerous weapons and explosives.

During a search of the records from the club on a secret computer, it was learned that the original owner, who later committed suicide, was the leader of an underground terror group and that there were plans to confront the secret service at the White House and make an entry. They had plans that showed where the possible weaknesses are and the type of dogs they had on the grounds. The plans had many high-powered guns and bombs that were to be used. The original club owner was known to the feds, but they never knew of his plans and personnel involved. This was a big find for the feds as this issue had many branches that would keep them busy for a while. Again, the club was closed down by the feds and many innocents put out of work.

The Hurt had gone through many changes as well as personnel and owners. The club was put in a receivership by the city and county and a real businessman put in charge. He did not own the club but would manage it to get it up and running smoothly and successfully and get people back to work. As this new overseer went through the club with a fine-tooth comb, he discovered secrets with the books and secret compartments within the building. He discovered a large hole covered up by many kitchen supplies. He summoned help to clear the area and saw that there was a large lock on a door. One of the helpers got a hammer and pried the lock from the door. Once opened it, they discovered a large stash of explosives. There was detonation cord, C-4, and dynamite. They immediately called the police and bomb squad. The club was evacuated, and upon the arrival of the police, they evacuated the surrounding areas near the club.

The bomb squad used their robot to get a better look and discovered a large stash that had not been seen before. Word got to the press, and many of the media showed up but had to stay at a distance. The bomb squad detectives then started to remove the explosives, and to their surprise, there were many photos. They called the FBI and ATF to assist in the find and investigation as this would definitely turn into a federal case. There were several photos of skinhead types, and the one that caught the eye of the police was one of the original owner of the club standing with some others holding what appeared to be hand grenades. This guy came off as such a nice guy, and unbeknownst to many was this insane background.

CHAPTER 9

But now the feds had photos of many others that were involved in the possession of the explosives. They would use facial recognition in an attempt to identify them and go forward with prosecution. The removal of all the explosives would take many hours because of the sheer amount. A few weeks after the removal of the explosives, they got several hits on the photos, and boy, were they stunned. They had the photo of not only the original owner of the club but also several past city officials. One of the city officials had died a short time ago, but another was still alive and living in the state. The FBI would go after him and charge him with possession of explosive materials and whatever else the feds came up with.

Word got to the city official that the FBI was looking for him, and he decided to leave where he was, in an attempt to disappear. But he was cornered by the feds and local police as he started to drive away from his residence. He saw the roadblock and quickly drove back to his home and barricaded himself inside. The police and FBI surrounded the home and called the SWAT team and bomb squad just in case there were explosives due to his past. The FBI negotiator arrived and, after a briefing, got on the phone with the suspect in an attempt to get him to come out. The suspect told the FBI that he was a changed man now and his past was just that—his past.

He said that he did not have any weapons or bombs but still would not come out. The FBI felt that this was a ruse to get the law enforcement to get close and then blow them up. The FBI then spoke with neighbors, and they were told that the suspect had spoken about bombs and his liking for seeing things blown up. This gave the FBI pause, and they decided to have a full square block evacuated as they felt that the suspect had explosives and would probably use them. SWAT snipers set up a block away with a shoot-to-kill order when they get the shot. The FBI did not want bloodshed but feared that if the suspect was cornered, he might blow the place up. The FBI did not want any law enforcement personnel killed.

The negotiator kept asking the sniper team if they were able to see anything, but they could not. The negotiator then told one of the perimeter officers to throw rocks on the roof and then the suspect would think someone was on the roof and maybe come to the window to check. The officer threw some rocks, and like clockwork, the suspect came to the window, then the crack of a rifle going off. The window shattered, and the suspect was killed with a head shot. The SWAT team slowly sent in the robot to look around, and no bombs were seen. The SWAT team made entry and cautiously searched the home along with a bomb dog. Nothing illegal was found; just like the suspect advised, several handguns were found but nothing illegal. The FBI and their evidence recovery team went in and stayed for several hours removing possible evidence.

The FBI went to the city administration to get the files on the dead ex-city official and see if he had contacts with anyone else. The FBI later learned that the city official had knowledge of two past club owners with mob ties. The FBI was really more interested in finding out how so much explosive material was hoarded inside the rock-and-roll club. This case now got the attention of Homeland Security and the White House.

They were thinking the worst, and as it turned out, there was worse. The city records tied into the club management that was supported by mob influence and, in turn, had contacts inside the Obama White House.

There was no evidence as yet tying the president to anything but to several high-ranking persons. The local police departments were being pushed out of the investigation now that Homeland Security was involved, because of its sensitivity. The feds could not believe that this little rock-and-roll club in South Florida had become of major interest to national security. The Washington press was now all over this inside Washington and in South Florida. Many national media outlets were camped outside the club in South Florida, trying to get someone to speak, but no one would come forward, fearing what the government might do to them. After a few days, the media disappeared as the story slowed down.

There was a group of white nationalists not happy with the government. Could this group be responsible for obtaining the explosives as this group was very radical and hated blacks and Black Lives Matter? In fact, it was later learned that there had been numerous thefts from large construction sites, where explosive materials had been stolen for over a year. Several from this group frequented the rock-and-roll club and befriended the owner and got him involved. They convinced him to store some explosive materials in the club for payment. And as more stolen explosives were obtained, they were stored at the club. They were living a very dangerous game, which could have caused a major explosion killing many hundreds. The Hurt was not the same, looking back on all the issues and problems with owners and staff, a fire and now this was unexplainable.

The person in charge from the courts had not been seen in over a week, and no one knew where he was. His cell phone went to voicemail, his residence looked OK, his car was gone, and no one knew where he might have gone. Unbeknownst to the courts and the feds, the radicals that still worked in The Hurt had been fortifying the club every night after closing. The staff was very quietly protecting the windows from any bullets, and the few doors were boarded up, with a small area to get in or out left open. The staff was secretly bringing in heavy weapons, gas masks, bulletproof vests, and a lot of ammo.

It was apparent that they were getting ready for a confrontation with the feds. Then it was learned that the court-appointed receiver was alive and was being kept in the basement of the club as a hostage because of the feds' interference in their business. After several nights, the club was fully fortified against any intrusion by the feds. The radical group of malcontents were willing to die for the cause. They were not even sure what the cause was, but they hated the federal government and law enforcement. Their bargaining chip was the court-appointed receiver of the club. Times were tense at the club. It had been shut down for what people believed were renovations, not knowing that it was being made into a fortress.

Now that the club was fully fortified with many weapons stored inside and holding hostage their one and only bargaining chip, the receiver appointed by the feds, they now waited for the feds to make a move, and just a few days later, the club personnel got their wish. It was leaked to the FBI that the federal hostage was being held in the basement and that the club was fortified and that the group inside had many weapons.

The FBI swat team took point on the case along with the ATF SWAT team. The local police departments took up positions on the outer perimeter, detouring traffic and handling evacuations. The FBI knew this was going to be a long standoff and brought buses in to move out those near the club. The police told the residents to gather some personal items and clothes and leave their homes. They were taken to a nearby hotel paid for by the feds.

A staging area was set up for the media and the agencies' spokesperson as there were many. News and law enforcement helicopters were hovering overhead, but their noise was making it had to hear on the ground, so they were told to move out of the area and film from a distance, which they did. The FBI made numerous attempts to contact anyone inside by phone, text, and bullhorn, but they had no response. The club personnel could stay inside for a long time as they had food and drink as well as an indoor generator for power just in case the electricity was shut off. But the FBI had no idea they had a generator so if they cut off the power, it would not matter. This went on for several days, with no one talking to each other.

The mayor of the city was sympathetic as to what was happening, but it was hurting the local businesses and causing major traffic problems. The mayor met with the FBI and asked if there was any way things could be made to move forward. The FBI told the mayor that they were working on a plan to get in but were worried about how many casualties there could be, as they did not want any. Another day went by without any movement, but then one of the aerial views showed a weakness: the vents on top of the building were open, giving the feds an opening. The decided to get on the roof and pump massive amounts of tear gas in, with the hope of the radicals coming out, but the gas would have to be put in very quickly as the group had gas masks.

Several SWAT members were able to get on the roof very quietly, and while that was happening, several other SWAT team members made noise at the front to draw their attention away from the roof. SWAT rapidly shot numerous canisters of very powerful tear gas into the roof vents, and the gas they used was highly effective and quick acting, so even if the radicals got to their gas masks, these would not help. The team almost immediately heard coughing and screaming. The team then got down from the roof and just waited to see if the doors would open and the radicals come out. They waited for several minutes but nothing.

Approximately five to ten minutes later, numerous gunshots were heard coming from inside the club. The SWAT team then reacted and used their SWAT vehicle with a battering ram attached and rammed the front door with such force that the doors came flying off the hinges. The team was behind the vehicle and cautiously made entry into the club, with their machine guns pointed and ready to shoot. As they made entry, they saw bodies around the front of the club. They searched and found no one alive; all had been shot and killed. A large handmade sign saying "long live rock and roll" had been hung on the wall. This was a sad ending to a once-popular rock-and-roll club in South Florida, or was it?

One of the SWAT officers was overheard saying, "At least we didn't have to kill them, although I wish we did." This comment did not go over well as the officer saying this was overheard by one of the victims' parents. The parent yelled out, "How dare you say that about my son?"

The officer turned toward the woman and said, "I'm glad your scumbag son is dead. He saved the taxpayers a lot of money," and then walked away. The woman was floored after hearing that and attempted to get the officer's name, but he walked away and no one else would tell her.

The city then ordered the club razed in the hopes of the city building a condo. But before that could happen, the city would have to hold a series of meetings, which would take months. But now there was interest by the police and fire department to get a loan and rebuild the club after it would be razed. The interested parties went before the commission and pleaded their case to rebuild the club after it came down and make it better and safer for the community. After numerous committees and commission meetings, the city granted the permits needed to rebuild. The time came when the building was imploded in front of many of those who worked there and partied there.

The surrounding areas were sealed off by the police, the demolition crew had set up the last charge, then the city mayor was given the task of hitting the button. After the countdown from 10 to 1, the mayor hit the button, and like clockwork, the explosions started one after the other until the building collapsed into itself. Then the fire department started to pump water onto the smoldering debris. The smell of gunpowder was in the air, and small particles of dust floated in the air. Then it was over; the once gamed and infamous Hurt club was no more. Many had tears in their eyes as they thought back to the good days from the past with all the concerts, new talent, and friendships.

It was a new day and new owners got the permits to rebuild, but this time a group of firefighters and others had become the new owners. Their plan was to create a new version of The Hurt rock club and start working on a new opening night of guests and bands. And of course, Johnny Depp would be contacted if he could make an appearance, which would really bring in the crowds. The new owners had previously decided they needed a better class of patrons and not the troubled rock groups. So they would institute a dress code and high cost to get in, as well as more expensive drinks.

Their new security personnel would have to be martial artists, not thugs, and know how to deal with people without being brutal. The bar staff would have to be very experienced, look good, and know the drinking laws of the city and state. The waitstaff would also have to be a certain look so they looked good in the uniform. The kitchen help and cooks would also have to be properly trained and look good. All personnel would go through an extensive background check as well as a driver's license check. There would be a valet service for the cars, and the valet service would be fully vetted, with background check and driver's license check. Off-duty police officers would be detailed at the club each night for a law enforcement presence on property. Nothing was left to chance this time; it had to be done correctly for the city to approve.

As the new owners were preparing for what they thought would be a great opportunity for them and the city, the demolition was ongoing. The demo crew were working pretty quickly when all of a sudden, a worker yelled out to the bulldozer operator, "Stop, stop, stop!" A supervisor came running over, asking what the problem was, and the worker said, "Look in the hole." Numerous human skeletal remains were scattered in the large pit. The demolition came to a halt, and the police were called in. Homicide detectives and crime scene arrived as the area was sealed off. Word got out to the new owners and to the media, who showed up in droves. The new owners could not believe what they saw and heard.

The bones were removed very carefully, which took several days. After the search was completed, the detectives and crime scene unit as well as the medical examiner removed twenty-five bodies, and what made it worse was that the bones were of children. This was huge news nationwide and again put the city in the limelight. After several months, many of the remains were identified as missing and abducted children from many years earlier, when a serial killer roamed the city back in the 1960s. The killer had died in prison but lived in a small home that was on the property before a business bought it and tore down the home and built a new building.

Apparently, the construction people did not dig down far enough to find the bones. Some of the bones could not be identified, but what was learned was that the bones had knife wounds, which were the apparent cause of death. So now the new owners had to put on hold the development of the new club indefinitely. Two of the foremen on the job were older men who had their daughters taken from them in a kidnapping and had little to no information on their case, which was over forty years old. As the bones were being removed, the two men spoke of their cases and how the finding of the bones would help the surviving family members of their dead kids.

The digging and collection of evidence continued and at the medical examiner's office; several of the bodies were able to be identified from newly tested DNA from cold cases from many years earlier. And then a blockbuster—two of the remains were that of the two foremen's missing girls. This information was given to the police, and they were told to bring the two men to the ME's office. The men were approached at the site and asked by the police to come with them and that the ME needed to talk with them. The men were a little perplexed but went with the officer. Upon their arrival at the ME's office, they were taken into a room and had the news broken to them that remains found at the club site were those of both men's daughters.

The men were stunned and speechless for several moments. Then they burst out crying. They consoled each other as the ME explained how the remains were identified. Now they could tell their families and have some closure. Unfortunately, one of the men's wives had died several years earlier of cancer, but the rest of the family would be at peace. Many others would be identified in time, and those families could get some closure. The new owners were mortified at what was discovered on their property and pledged a large donation to a fund for missing and exploited children.

As the digging continued at the crime scene site, a business card was discovered, belonging to the original owner of the club, Big Bob. But to everyone's surprise, it was not the Big Bob everyone knew but his father, from many, many years ago. It turned out that he was a notorious serial killer of children. Big Bob never told anyone about his father's past and maybe it was the reason he purchased The Hurt; we will never know.

The scene was now cleared and turned over to the new owners to start building the new club. The build was going very well, on time and under budget. Approximately six months later, the club was finished, and it was the state of the art: a great sound system, big kitchen, separate offices for the owners, four great big restrooms, ticket office at the front door, and twenty-five well-trained and vetted bouncers that knew martial arts. A grand opening was set up, and many government dignitaries were invited, such as the mayor, police chief, fire chief, and the city commissioners. The night of the grand opening, many police officers were on scene for crowd control and traffic control.

A couple of searchlights were out and operational as well as many media outlets. There would be a second grand opening where many rock-and-roll bands and celebrities will be on hand. The first grand opening went on without incident. The place was packed; all the staff looked great and acted very professional. The food was great, and the drinks were flowing. As the night went on and the club thinned out, the owners were congratulated by the city officials as well as the police and fire chiefs. The owners felt great and were very happy that they put this event together in their new club.

A few weeks later, the second grand opening occurred, and again the club was packed with several celebrities and up-and-coming rock-and-roll bands. To everyone's surprise, a guest appearance was mad by Johnny Depp. Only the club owners knew Johnny was coming as they wanted it to be a big surprise, and boy, was it. As the night progressed, one of the owners went on stage to thank everyone for coming and then said, "We have a special guest to also thank you." Then the band played on a dark stage, and a minute later, the spotlight went on and lit up a guy with his back to the audience; he then slowly turned around, and the club went absolutely crazy. Johnny spoke into the mic and welcomed everyone. The crowd was still screaming and clapping for Johnny's appearance. He then picked up his guitar and played a set with the band, which took about forty-five minutes.

After he was done, he thanked everyone and left the stage to a loud cheer. He went backstage to leave and met with the owners, who were very grateful he showed up. Johnny then left the club via his limo and was escorted by the police to the airport. The club crowd was still talking about Johnny's appearance until the club closed. The second grand opening was also great.

The media gave the club a terrific write-up in the papers and on the local news. This state-of-the-art club got the attention of a TV production company that was looking for a venue for a new TV show it was producing. The club was advertised in the publication called *Variety*, a famous paper for production companies and movie stars.

The club owners got a call from one of the production companies in the paper, and producers flew out to meet the owners. When the producers got to the club, they were in awe of the place. It had everything the production company was looking for and more. After several meetings, the club owners and producers agreed on a contract to film a new TV show mostly at the club, and it was very lucrative too. The club owners got together and discussed the possible venture with their attorneys and agreed that it was a great deal. The producers were also well versed on the history of the club and floated the possibility of a movie based on the club's history. This also intrigued the club owners, who were going to give it much thought.

The owners were thinking that if a TV show was produced at the club, it would make the club a lot of money and put the place on the map. So after a few weeks and speaking with the lawyers, the owners decided to approve the proposition by the production company and permit the filming. The producers visiting stayed for a week, watching the operation nightly, and they were extremely impressed by the professionalism the staff and owners showed as well as the stage performances. The producers met and spoke with the law enforcement working the club and got a rave review advising that the club was professionally run, without any incidents. This information pleased the production team as they did not want any problems for their actors and crew.

The producers also met with the city leaders to explain the type of show being produced. The city leaders were fine with it but wanted the filming to show the city in a good light by featuring the beaches and downtown revitalization areas. The producers said, "No problem and that's what we also do when we film in a city." Everyone was anxious for the start of the filming, but there was much work to do. The club's lawyers got with the film production company to finalize the paperwork, which took approximately two weeks. The club would get a slight makeover and name change for the TV show, along with a few minor interior changes. The production execs also agreed to keep the staff on for the show, but they had to get legal paperwork completed for their pay and insurance.

The show would pay the staff $500 per episode, with a guarantee of at least fifteen episodes. All the staff were very excited and couldn't wait to get started. A few weeks later, a notice was put in the paper, for extras for the TV show as well as mentioning that the regular operation of the club would be suspended because of the filming. A week before the first rehearsal, the staff was fitted for their uniforms and their responsibilities. The newly hired director was a familiar face in Hollywood and had much experience with TV show productions. He met the staff and was very nice and cordial as he explained what he was looking for from them. The staff was very understanding and anxious to start.

CHAPTER 10

It was now time for rehearsal; the staff showed up, looking great in their uniforms, and they were given a script to review but they were mostly told to just react to the situation and not play to the cameras. The rehearsal went great, and the director was very happy with the staff since they had no professional training. An unfortunate byproduct of the new TV show was that the neighborhood was locked out from attending the club, but they were given opportunities to be extras in the club during the filming. There were restrictions and background checks required. Most were fine with this, but there were some troublemakers that felt it was not fair; some even traveled from far away to come to this new exciting rock-and-roll club.

They made formal complaints to the city and to the production company and wanted their money back for their trips from where they came from. This complaint fell on deaf ears as the request was very ridiculous. This complaining group was from Minneapolis and was antifa. This was a known domestic terror group that was just looking to destroy. There were only five of these disrupters, but they started to organize others to join the group. After a few days, the group had grown exponentially and it was more vocal. They started to be disruptive by blocking access to the club and yelling over bullhorns at the cast and crew.

The police were on scene and attempted to quell the disturbance but were met with rocks and bottles. Reinforcements were quickly brought in, and the group was arrested and jailed on felony charges. The police chief was very strong when it came to dealing with the antifa mob. Luckily the state attorney was also hard with the antifa thugs and got indictments on numerous felonies. The TV producers were very grateful to the police and prosecutors as they continued their production. The mayor was made aware of the antifa arrests and came out very strong against them; this story got out and went national, right up to the White House and Oval Office, which got the president to call the mayor and congratulate him on what he had done. The president even made a comment that he might come to see the mayor and the club.

Word got back to the club owners that the president might decide to come to town to see the club and the mayor. This information really excited the club owners and staff as they were all supporters of this president. The FBI was able to arrest many antifa wannabes, and after a while, they went away and never returned, mainly because of the city government not tolerating their criminal antics like many other liberal governments were doing. Months later, the club was visited by the police chief with some very cool news. The president of the United States was coming to visit in about a month, but the exact day had not been released as of yet by the Secret Service. The club owners got the staff together and told them about the impending presidential visit. "The Secret Service will be conducting background checks on all of us. They will also be setting up a security checkpoint before entering the club as well as locking down the entire area. So when we get the date, be prepared with a clean uniform. The police will be bringing in a K-9 to search for bombs, ammo, and narcotics, so do not bring anything inside the club or your cars."

The next day, the club got the date of the visit, and the security details arrived to start their checks. The president's assistant press secretary spoke with the club staff and told them that the president would allow pictures with him and would autograph hats and posters. But they should remember his security detail would be close. A few days later, the day that they waited for arrived. It was approximately 7:00 p.m. All the staff was in place; the security checkpoint was put in place by the advance agents.

The local police had the area locked down. The media mob had gathered out front, police helicopters were overhead, and a no-fly zone was established. Protesters located themselves a few blocks away and out of sight of the president. One of the Secret Service agents then told the club owners that the president just landed in Fort Lauderdale and should be here shortly. The club and surrounding areas got one last security sweep with the K-9, and the Secret Service snipers had taken their positions outside. Approximately twenty minutes later, the motorcade started to pull up, escorted by numerous police motorcycles and security vehicles. The president's limo pulled up, and the agents got out and took their positions.

The president exited and walked to the front of the club and greeted the city officials, mayor, governor, police and fire chiefs as well as the club's owners. After a few minutes, the president entered the very clean and fancy rock-and-roll club and greeted the staff. There was loud clapping and yelling to the president, "Four more years." The president was smiling, and he shook hands with all and took photos. He was then escorted around the club and then taken to a large table, where he sat with the city officials and club owners. They discussed the recent events about antifa and how they were handled by the law enforcement and city officials. The president was given an iced tea, and after approximately forty-five minutes, he had to leave. He thanked everyone and took a group photo with all the club staff.

They all thanked him for coming and yelled out, "God bless you, Mr. President." He then gave several fist pumps and got into his limo. The security then took their positions and the motorcycle cops started the escort back to the airport and *Air Force One*. Once the motorcade was gone, the club staff stayed then celebrated and with a few drinks. They were all still in amazement that the president was there. They all had their pictures with the president and autographs on many different items.

The club owners kept the chair and table that the president sat in at a special location. They had a glass partition surrounding it for protection as the chairs had the presidential seal on them and no one was to sit on them. This was the club's showpiece. A picture of the table and chairs was put in the local magazine. This was a large draw for the patrons as they liked to have their picture taken near it since it was probably the only time they would get that close to a president.

Soon after, several reporters came to the club to interview the owners about the presidential visit. When the reporters arrived and started their questioning, it was very apparent they were not fans of the president. The questions were gotcha questions and ridiculous. After a few minutes, the owners had enough and asked the reporters to leave. It turned out that one of the reporters turned out to be reportedly antifa and working for their magazine. It was unclear if the magazine had this knowledge or not. But in today's world, anything was possible. The owners knew what this group was all about and felt that this guy might be summing up the place for a future attack. He knew they loved their cops and the president, and he and his fucked-up group of criminals did not. This made the owners worried, so they installed more twenty-four-hour camera surveillance, cameras that were protected against damage or from being spray-painted. They also hired extra vetted armed security for the club after hours, meaning they hired off-duty cops for an off-duty detail after their shifts; the cops loved it because for them it was easy money and they knew the club owners took care of them. The money was pretty good, $40 per hour with a four-hour minimum.

At the start of their new police detail, they were given their orders by one of the owners. The two officers were to be vigilant as to who is lurking around or loitering around the property. Identify and arrest them if they are loitering, as charges would be pressed. The officers were very familiar with antifa and had no problem dealing with them. The first few weeks, the officers had no interactions with anyone as things were calm. This kept the owners happy as they did not want any issues with their very new and famous club. They even took care of the cops if they wanted to come in off duty with their families or on duty for lunch, as they were never charged.

One particular night, several off-duty officers were in the club with their wives when one of the owners came over to them. He asked if everything was OK and was told yes, thank you. The owner then asked if he could speak to the officer away from his family. The officer got up and walked with the owner to the front of the club. The owner told the officer that there was a guy inside at one of the tables, sitting with another guy and girl. He said, "It's the same guy that was the reporter that came here a few weeks back for a story and he was antifa. Back then, I told him to get out, and now he is here. What a scumbag. Would it be possible for you to be with me as he has to leave?"

The officer said, "Sure can." The owner then told his bouncers of the issue and to be alert that they were going to ask some guy to leave and it might not go well. The owner also notified his outside security of the issue and told them to be alert as he did not know if this antifa fuck would cause a problem along with his friend.

The owner and the officer then walk up to the table, where the owner looked at the subject and said, "Do you remember me?"

The guy said, "Yes, we spoke during our short interview for the magazine."

The owner said, "Correct, and you need to leave, so pay your bill and depart, please. The guy asked why and was told, "It's the same reason you were asked to leave last time, so pay up and leave, and you're not allowed back here." And this was being said in front of this officer, who identified himself. The guy was not happy and told the officer and owner to fuck off as he paid his check and left with his friend. They were followed out to the front and watched by the front-door bouncers and outside security. As they got onto the sidewalk and started to walk away from the front door, the owner and officer turned away to go back inside.

Then two loud bangs pierced the night's air and the owner fell to the ground, then several loud bangs as the subject also fell to the ground. The unarmed security took cover, as did others near the door. The club owner had been shot, and just after that, the officer returned fire and shot the subject. It was now chaos at this new club. No one else was hurt, luckily. The crime scene was small, but no one could come in or out through the front door. Some of the bouncers told the patrons inside, "Because of an emergency, the club has to close and you have to leave through the back door, and if you owe a check, tonight's food and drinks are on us." Luckily, the club was not too busy and emptied fairly quickly.

The police and fire rescue were called as the officer tended to his friend the owner. Luckily, the bullets did not hit any major organs and were fairly superficial. He was able to control the bleeding and told the owner he would be OK; the officer then went to check on the suspect, to find him deceased. Upon arrival of the police and medics, the owner was tended to, then transported to the hospital; the police sealed off the front of the club as the suspect's body was covered up. The friend never ran as he was totally surprised at his friend's actions. He stayed on scene to be interviewed by detectives. The officer's wife was stunned that their night out, away from the kids, turned into a nightmare. The officer's wife was told to go home as her husband would be on scene for a while.

The homicide unit was now on scene and spoke to all involved but quickly got out after they heard that there might be some trouble brewing. The dead suspect was taken to the medical examiner for autopsy.

The other club owner, who was off this night, was called, and he responded very quickly to the club and once there to see his staff he went to the hospital where his partner was being treated. After the scene was cleared by all and the staff closed up the club, the suspect's friend had made a few calls to his other antifa buddies and told them, "A cop killed our brother for no reason," which was not true. This information was obtained by the police department's intel unit very quickly. The police chief, now fearing a riot, mobilized his troops and told them to report with all their riot gear and less lethal weapons. As many officers were en route to the club area, officers called in that they were passing numerous cars and trucks with what appeared to be antifa, as most were wearing full face masks and helmets. Antifa was well organized and well-funded by the Democrats.

The chief called the sheriff's office and spoke with the sheriff. The chief asked for mutual aid assistance, and the sheriff of course said yes, and would have at least three to five hundred deputies geared up and ready to respond. The media got word of a potential confrontation and had their reporters and live trucks go out to the scene. The antifa group started to assemble a block from the club, and it was getting fairly large. Many officers were now in place around the club and in their riot gear. Other officers blocked off several surrounding streets to the club also. Then a large caravan of deputy sheriffs started to arrive and bolstered the officers at the club and set up their formation to move out the antifa group. Hundreds of deputies were now on scene under their own command.

They outnumbered the antifa group three to one. They were in their riot gear with shields and less lethal weapons. Several lines of deputies were in front, and behind them several K-9 units and behind them were commanders and more deputies. They started to move in formation down the street, basically surrounding the antifa group and started to take some frozen water bottles and rocks. The deputies threw flash-bangs and used tear gas as they got closer, even making numerous arrests. Fortunately, no deputies were injured. The rest of antifa were forced back into their trucks and cars as they then fled the area yelling, "We will be back, we are coming back!" Those arrested were taken to jail on numerous felony charges and given high bails. The deputies stayed on scene through the night just in case antifa came back, but none did, so the deputies departed with the thanks from the police chief. The police officers mostly departed also with a small contingent left around the club until morning.

This was a wake-up call to the new club owners, fearing that their place would be a flashpoint for violence and destruction. The owners spent more money for security, placing two guards on the roof so they could get a better look at who was approaching the club. The owners also had a very strong metal fence built around the club with big gates that locked. There were pole cameras at the top of the fence that were motion activated. A guard dog was also kept on the property just in case someone made it inside the fenced area. Over the next few weeks, the security was reporting to the owners that they saw a white van drive by several times each week. The guards called the police, but nothing could be done as they only saw a white van driving, which was not illegal.

Whoever did the vetting of the security personnel did not do a good job. Two of the security personnel working the club had friends in the antifa mob and believed in what they did. It was believed that because of the past incident at the club when the owner got shot, their retribution was not ending. Then one night, one of the guards on the roof shot and killed the patrol dog. The guard then called his friend who was driving that white van to crash through the gate of the club. Then things happened very quickly. The guards on the roof came down and opened the door to the club. The van crashed through the gate, causing a lot of damage to the van and destroying the gate entrance. The guy in the van then got out with gasoline bombs and set them off throughout the club.

The two guards then got into the van with their friends and quickly departed. As they drove off, they could see the massive flames coming from the club. As they got a few blocks away, they see fire trucks heading the other way toward the club. Then numerous police cars also headed that way. By the time the fire department got there to fight the fire, the club was destroyed. The police found the dead dog near the gate with a bullet wound. This was obviously a targeted attack the antifa was trying to do. The police chief felt the feds should be involved as he too believed that antifa was the cause. So he called the FBI in to assist with the investigation.

As the suspects fled the scene, a police officer was driving by and saw a white van drive by. He was the officer who took a report of a white van driving around the club days earlier. He had a gut feeling and got behind the van as it sped away. The officer activated his emergency lights in an attempt to pull the van over, but the van would not stop. The officer called it in over the radio and advised he was in pursuit of the possible arson suspects. He chased the van for approximately ten minutes until it took a turn too fast and flipped over. Two of the suspects were ejected and killed; the other two were still in the van, unconscious. Numerous other officers were now on scene as well as paramedics. The two killed were the security guards from the club.

The paramedics were able to get the other two out of the van and onto gurneys, to which the police handcuffed them. The suspects were taken to the hospital under heavy guard as the FBI took over. The medical examiner was on scene to check on the dead suspects.

Meanwhile, the club owners responded and could not believe their eyes. The club was a total loss. They were heartbroken after all they did to make this club a hit. They started to cry and console each other. They then went to the police station to speak with detectives and the FBI. The two suspects that survived had tattoos on them that said "antifa forever." They were not hurt very badly as the FBI was there to speak with them, but they lawyered up very quickly.

One of the police detectives had one of the suspects alone in the hospital room and started to ask questions, but the suspect failed to respond, only saying, "Fuck off."

The detective said, "What did you say?"

The suspect said, "I said fuck off. Are you deaf?" The detective shut the room door and started to tune this guy up. The detective said, "Your fucking group of haters destroyed my good friends' livelihood and did a great disservice to the community, and I'm glad your two friends died in the crash." The detective then took the oxygen tube and bent it to reduce the oxygen flow. The suspect was gasping for air then the detective released the bend and asked if the suspect was ready to talk.

Again, the words "fuck off" were spewed. Again, the detective bent the tube and held it longer this time until the suspect was begging for air. Unfortunately, a nurse walked in, so the detective had to cool it. The detective's partner then came into the room and said, "We have to go. Something came up." They walked out of the room, and on the way out, the detective turned to the suspect in bed and told him, "I will be back." One of the detectives got word that they received chatter picked up by the FBI that antifa was going to be targeting the detectives' homes and families due because of what happened to their friends.

Knowing that antifa usually keeps their word, the detectives and other officers involved in the previous chase that killed some of their members were worried. Those officers involved had to tell their families to leave and go to another family's home until things calmed down. This was very unfair as the children had to be moved around during the school year, but it was a necessary evil. The police department also had extra patrols around the officers' homes.

The following day, the police chief was notified by the FBI that they needed to have a meeting with all the police brass ASAP. Later in the afternoon, the police and FBI met and were told that the FBI had undercover agents with the local antifa and that they were stockpiling weapons for a targeted assault, but the location was unknown at this time. The FBI special agent in charge would get all up to speed as soon as he heard anything. This was a little unsettling for the police chief as he feared that one of his guys was the target. The next day, a police officer was not at the roll call, which started at 7:00 a.m. Calls were made to his phone, and an officer went to the home.

Upon the officer's arrival at the home, nothing looked out of order.

The front door was locked, the officer's car was in the driveway, but when the responding officer went around back, he saw the letters ACAB (all cops are bastards) spray-painted on the rear wall. The responding officer then decided that there might be something wrong and requested a backup along with the fire department to make an entry. The fire department responded and broke open the front door for the officers to get in; the firemen stayed back. Several officers cautiously entered and started to search for the missing officer. As they walked through the house, they were yelling his name, "Scott, Scott!" but no response.

As the officers went up to the second floor, they entered the master bedroom, where they found the officer and his wife dead from what appeared to be stab wounds. ACAB was painted over the walls; they now had a double homicide probably involving antifa. The antifa thugs had been known to go after any law enforcement person that came after them. This was a fear presented by the police chief. The chief immediately put out a memo to all his troops that patrol would now have two officers in the car and that when off duty and home, they must secure all the windows and locks to the house as well as the cars. When the crime scene unit was at the deceased officer's home, they did not discover anything other than the bodies.

Then a call came in that the thugs were downtown and around the site of The Hurt club, gathering and handing out different types of weapons. Undercover in the crowd were plainclothes officers that got word out that the group was going to the local jail and police department main office. Antifa got a fix by destroying police stations and setting fires. Back at the police station, the captured antifa thug was singing away and spilling his guts. This guy stated that his antifa buddies wanted to take over the site of The Hurt and turn it into a shrine for their fallen brothers, but the city wanted nothing to do with this and did not permit the antifa to build anything there, especially on the site of the great rock-and-roll club.

CHAPTER 11

The club owners pooled their money in an effort to keep the antifa from doing anything on the club site. But in typical fashion, antifa got with BLM and protested outside the city commissioners' homes as well as the club owners for interfering with what the antifa wanted to do. During one of the so-called peaceful protests, someone in the crowd started throwing objects at one of the homes of the club owners. There were approximately fifty to seventy-five protesters out front, and others started throwing rocks and frozen bottles through the windows. Now the club owner, fearing for his safety and that of his wife and kids, decided to return the favor. Remember this owner was a city fireman. But now as he was personally under attack and his business burned down by this mob, he had had it.

He then made the decision to take revenge on anyone in his sights. He then made a decision that would change his life and that of his family. He told his wife to take his two young kids to a safe room as he retrieved his AR-15 rifle and a lot of ammo. He loaded the gun by attaching his thirty-round magazine and took aim. Then as the crowd was chanting and using bullhorns, loud multiple bangs were heard. People were dropping and others scattering and taking cover. As many lay on the ground and hid behind parked cars, numerous bullets were coming their way and finding their targets. Then silence. A few minutes went by as those hiding started to get up, at which time more gunfire and many more victims. Then in the background, multiple sirens were heard and getting closer.

As many lay dead and dying, the police were getting closer; the police carefully approached as they still encountered gunshots. Then a woman's voice screamed from inside the house, "Don't kill him, don't kill him!" But as the officers made a tactical approach, they too came under fire from the shooter in the house. The police called for a negotiator even though the suspect had a mass killing. The negotiator arrived as the scene was secured. The SWAT team used their armored vehicle to get the wounded out to safety, and there were many.

The negotiator from the police department actually knew the shooter as they worked out together. The negotiator knew that the suspect had suffered a great loss through antifa burning down his business. He knew that the suspect and his fellow firemen lost a lot the night of the fire, but this was not the answer. The suspect just lost it and felt this was the only way to move forward, taking out his enemies that threatened him and his family. The negotiator had also summoned the suspect's co-owners of the club in an effort to talk him out. They all took turns talking and pleading with him to come out and to let his family out first unharmed. The suspect kept yelling, "I'm happy what I did! They needed to be dead, just like they killed me." After approximately three hours, the suspect had his wife and two kids leave the home. He yelled out, "My wife and kids are coming out!"

The front door opened, and the family slowly exited and then was swiftly taken to safety and away from the scene. The wife then spoke with the SWAT commander, telling him that her husband lost his mind after what that group did to his dreams. "He knows that he will not come out alive, but please don't kill the father of my children."

Then the front door opened, and the suspect appeared, still carrying the rifle. He yelled out, "I'm sorry, and tell my kids I love them!" He then walked swiftly from the front door to the front yard and pointed his rifle at the SWAT team, then several of them fired multiple rounds at the suspect, killing him. This was a suicide-by-cop scenario.

The suspect's firemen friends were beyond devastated. They remembered their friend as a kind, compassionate good guy and great family man. But they knew when he lost everything to antifa, he had to do something. The suspect lay dead in his front yard as the SWAT team walked up on him and handcuffed him. The suspect's wife was devastated and had to be taken to the hospital with her young kids. She was met at the hospital by the fire chief and police chief. They both were extremely upset over this incident. Back at the scene, the suspect got his revenge; he had killed over fifteen antifa and wounded many more. As the crime scene unit started their work, they found many firearms on the dead terrorists. Now there were many media outlets on the scene, and this was a national story. Even the president of the United States commented. He was very saddened to hear what had happened and promised his administration would vigorously go after antifa and any other homegrown terror group.

Several days later, the fire department brass asked the city for a funeral for a fallen fireman. The city said no because the suspect, a city fireman, became a mass murderer. The fire chief pleaded with the mayor, saying, "Because the suspect was a city fireman, he gave his all to the city, and because of the antifa taking away his livelihood, we should not diminish what the fireman has done for the city."

The mayor said, "Sorry, no. We cannot celebrate the life of a mass murderer."

The chief was very hurt, so he went back to the rank and file and told them that the funeral would be a normal one without all the fanfare given to a fallen fireman. Many of the department's fire personnel then decided to call out sick, leaving the city very short-handed, so the mayor reached out to the county sheriff to fill the loss.

But in solidarity, the county fire department refused to go. This got to the city commission and to the community meeting, where the residents told the mayor to permit the upgraded funeral and that we know why the fireman committed the mass killing, but this has nothing to do with a big funeral. But the mayor stood his ground and denied the request. Then a huge fire in a warehouse broke out, and because of the lack of firemen, the warehouse was a total loss as well as some nearby vehicles. Well, the warehouse owner was furious and filed a lawsuit against the city and fire department. Now the mayor was under a lot of pressure, and he felt that he would be kicked out of office or lose his re-election.

So after much thought he caved in and permitted the upgraded funeral, to the delight of many. Days later, the funeral was held with hundreds in attendance. It was very smooth and without any protests. But the media was terrible with their headlines: "Fireman goes to hell," "Murdering fireman not charged." The mayor had to declare a state of emergency and summoned fire units from surrounding counties, but after the mayor changed his mind, the fire department came back to work but to a furious community. The two other fireman club owners received insurance money from the destroyed club and decided to rebuild but not as a club but a memorial to the lives lost and to their friend who committed suicide. This did not sit well with antifa and the BLM group, they put out a statement saying, "It's not over."

The memorial got the approval of the city leaders and mayor as well as most of the community. The memorial would have tributes to the club and what it did for the city and those involved in its rebuilding. The good and the bad would be on display. The owners felt that the public should see the entire picture and history of the site and club. Things were calm in the city, and after many weeks, it was business as usual. The city was quiet, people working the police and fire departments on duty, and the memorial was in its first stage of building. The club owners were always believers in second chances and hired a few guys who were antifa and left that life as it was going nowhere except to prison or the cemetery. So these guys were hired to help in the rebuild.

As time went on, these two guys (let's call them ex-antifa) seemed to be working out fine. They showed up when needed and didn't bother anyone else on the site. But their former group would come by and harass them for leaving the group. They were yelling and cursing at the ex-antifa. The last thing shouted was "You will see what happens for leaving." The ex-antifa just blew it off as they heard this before. A few days later in the early morning with the sun rising, a few workers came to the building site and discovered two bodies on the site. It was the two ex-antifa, and it looked like they were shot multiple times. The police and crime scene unit responded along with the two firemen/owners. They were devastated by what had happened.

There was a note on top of one of the deceased and it stated, "We told you." This was a good lead for the homicide detectives as they had many witnesses to who had come by and made the threats. But it would not be easy finding the suspects as antifa had a good way of hiding people. The forensic unit made a great discovery: one of the victims had a necklace in his closed fist, and it had pictures of a young man and woman. The victim probably grabbed the suspect during the fight and pulled off the necklace without the suspect knowing. The homicide unit had that picture blown up to an 8″ × 10″ and showed it around the neighborhood. When they walked into a gay club, they met with the owner, and he was shown the photo. As soon as he looked at it, a weird look came on his face.

He then sat down at a table, just staring at the photo. He started to cry and covered his face and then said, "That's Mike." The detectives asked who Mike was, and they were told that Mike was his son. The detectives asked where Mike could be found, and his father told them he had not seen Mike in several weeks and did not know where he was. They asked if he had any affiliation with known terror groups. The father said he did not know but felt that something might be wrong as Mike's demeanor changed when he spoke with him. The detectives asked if Mike owned any firearms, and they were told, "Yes, he did, he had a 9-mm and .38 handgun." The detectives give the father a business card and tell him to call if he heard from him. The detectives leave and are very suspicious, so they put a tap on the father's phone.

As the detectives left, they saw the father go to the phone on the counter and they felt that they were lied to and that he was calling his son to warn him. The detectives went back to their office and got a printout of the tap they had on the father's phone. And just as they thought, the father immediately made a call to a local number. The detective traced the call to a rooming house in town. They got a search and arrest warrant for that property and had the SWAT team deliver it.

The next night, the SWAT team and homicide detective went to the rooming house and executed the warrants. They went to the desk clerk and showed the picture of the suspect and asked what room he was in. At first, the clerk denied that the suspect was there, but then the homicide detective told him, "If you're lying, you're going to prison." The clerk caved and told them the room number. SWAT was in the lead as the detectives stayed back. The SWAT leader knocked then broke in the door and threw a flash-bang into the room. They entered and found the suspect dead from a gunshot wound to the head, and self-inflicted. In the room, they also found newspaper clippings of the double homicide at the club site. There was a picture of the suspect with an unknown girl on the dresser, and in the picture, you could see the necklace that was found in the hand of the murder victim.

This looked like the double murder was almost solved, but there were two suspects. The dead suspect, Mike, had a laptop computer that was taken by the homicide detectives. The crime scene unit responded and took control of the scene as other officers sealed off the scene. The homicide detectives took the computer to their computer crimes unit, and they believed they had found the other suspect, seen in pictures on the computer. There were many pictures of the suspects together in many parts of the city. The pictures were time-stamped, and you could see the necklace in the pictures. In one picture time-stamped just a few days before the double murder, they were holding handguns, with the caption "let's get 'em."

Now the search was on for the second suspect. His picture was put all over the place by the police. The airports and seaports were also notified. Then the next day, the FBI got a tip from a TSA agent at the local airport. The tip was on the second murder suspect, and he was seen in the airport, working at a gift shop. This was relayed to the airport police and local FBI. Numerous airport cops and FBI sealed the area off and evacuated anyone nearby. They then sent in several undercover detectives looking like tourists. As they entered the business, they saw their suspect stacking the shelves. Then the detectives tackle the suspect to the ground yelling, "Police! Don't resist." They got the suspect handcuffed as the scene was sealed off.

The suspect was taken to a holding area in the airport and then handed off to the homicide detectives. The detectives then walked to their car, which was in front of the airport, and placed the suspect in the backseat along with one of the detectives. They drove away and went through town on the way to police headquarters. As they drive down a windy barren road, a dark SUV came up very quickly from behind and made an aggressive move around the detective's car. As the SUV pulled alongside the detective's car, the passenger in the SUV rolled his window down and stuck the barrel of a rifle out the window. Numerous gunshots rang out in rapid succession.

Many bullets hit the detective's car, at which time the car went out of control and off the road, into a ditch. The SUV then quickly left the area. A truck passing by saw the car in the ditch but saw nothing else. He got out and immediately saw three dead bodies, two in the back and one behind the wheel. He was in shock, as he never saw anything like this. He called 911 and gave the information and waited for the police. The scene was blocked off for investigators and the crime scene unit. The officers on scene then determined that two of the occupants were police detectives from their office. Now the top command was on scene and realized that the two detectives were escorting a suspect in the ongoing double murder involving antifa.

The command saw numerous bullet holes in the vehicle, and now they felt that this was an antifa hit; as they did not want the suspect to talk, they silenced him. But how did they know the suspect was being picked up and taken to the police station—possibly a leak but by whom? The command had a lot of questions but no answers.

The FBI was called in to help with the investigation. This investigation had grown into a massive one. Murder of two law enforcement detectives and the murder of a state witness was a big deal in not only the state but also the country.

The feds were now planning a massive takedown of antifa, but some Democrats didn't like this idea as it might result in innocent people being grabbed up and jailed. As usual, the Dems were not too concerned with the law-abiding citizens but feel for the criminal anarchists. While this was going on, the funerals for the detectives were moving forward, and the families decided to have a funeral for both detectives at the same time, then the bodies would go to their separate cemeteries for a private service. This incident got all the way to the White House and to the president, and he was so moved that he would be in attendance at the large funeral.

The families very much welcomed the president and knew he would speak at the funeral. He was a true backer of all law enforcement. Now the Secret Service had come in for the advance security for the funeral participants.

Security checkpoints were established, and the local and state law enforcement would be there in force as well. Because of the pandemic, all would be required to wear a mask and get tested before coming into the church. Everyone was fine with this protocol. The day of the funeral, the police chief posthumously promoted the detectives to first grade, which meant a larger monetary benefit for the families. The church was filling up fast after they went through the security checkpoint and COVID test. Everyone had to be in place before the president arrived, as his security footprint was very large.

The motorcade arrived, and the president was escorted in by his Secret Service team. He took a seat in the front row near the grieving families and greeted them individually, telling them how sorry he was for their incredible loss and the loss to the country. But there was no social distancing because of the large number of family and friends in a small church. There was a large piece of plexiglass in front of the podium. The President spoke first and was introduced by the Parish priest. He said, "Fellow parishioners, thank you for being here today for our fellow families and to mourn these two great guardians of the peace. And I am extremely honored to introduce the president of the United States, the Honorable Donald J. Trump." There was loud applause as the president took the podium.

His speech would be short so as to not take time away from the families who came to speak on the fallen hero's behalf. The president told the families, "Heaven is a safer place now, and you should be proud." After approximately ten minutes of pleasantries and how disgusted he felt about how law enforcement was viewed and attacked on a daily basis, the president told the crowd that he was a huge fan of law enforcement and would do everything in his power to protect our law enforcement. He then thanked everyone for letting him come here and say a few words. The president left the stage and spoke with the families a few moments and then departed the church. The funeral service went on for another few hours, as some family members spoke as the two fallen officers lay in their flag-draped caskets in front of the stage.

When the funeral ended, the caskets were escorted out by the police honor guards and placed into the hearse while the pipe-and-drum corps played. There were separate burials for the families as they were buried in different locations. Each hearse had numerous motorcycles as an escort; it was quite a sight. At the cemetery, the honor guards removed the caskets and walked them to the grave site, then a police helicopter flyover, followed by a bugler playing taps, then a prayer as the casket was placed into the gravesite as the family members cried. Then it was over, and everyone departed and hugged one another. Several weeks later, the fallen officers had their names engraved on the wall of heroes. But after all this, the left-wing media played it up and showed support for the cop killer because they felt the police should have protected him better. They showed their true stripes—fuck the police and the law-abiding citizens.

Then a bombshell from the forensic unit: after examining the bullets and shell casings, they had a hit in the data base from a previous police-involved shooting many months earlier. The bullets were matched up to the officer that was involved in a shooting in the past. This same officer was still on the force. Could this be the gunman who killed the detectives and the antifa member? This information was made available to the FBI and police chief.

Because of the nature of the murders, the FBI took the lead in the investigation. Quietly they obtained all the reports and records of the earlier police shooting to include all forensics, interviews, photos, and personal information on the officer involved. That also included all the social media accounts the officer had, and he was on all of them: Google, Facebook, Tinder, LinkedIn, Instagram, and a few others. The social media accounts had vague, cryptic messages from the shooting that he was involved in, and it made the hairs stand on the heads of the FBI. The FBI then started to look into the officer's friends and family discreetly and discovered that several of them had ties to radical group, one being antifa. So now the FBI felt that were on to something, and they told the police chief, "We believe the officer under investigation may have ties to antifa, but do not let anyone know you have this information as of yet. When we call the officer in, you will be notified and will sit in on the interrogation."

After a few weeks of finalizing all the FBI investigative reports, it was time to call in the suspect officer. The day the FBI went to the officer's home was the officer's day off. But when they looked in through an open window, they were surprised to see the place in disarray, so they called the fire department to gain access, and upon entering, they discovered alcohol bottles thrown all over, along with beer cans and blood on the kitchen floor. As the FBI walked through the home, they discovered the officer in the hallway off the kitchen dead from a self-inflicted gunshot wound to the head.

They then found a suicide note on the kitchen table. The note basically said "I found out you were looking at me for the triple murders and did not want to bring any trouble to my fellow antifa, so I took one for the team. I was affiliated with them for several years and believed in their cause. But you now must realize there is a mole in the police department, good luck." Now the FBI backed out of the crime scene and called for their evidence recovery unit. The FBI called the chief and told them what they found, and at first, there was silence then the chief asked if there was a suicide note and was told, "Yes, but we have a bigger problem." The FBI now believed that the conspiracy ran much deeper and closer to the command.

The FBI called in more special agents to sift through the social media of the entire police department, including the command staff. They put a freeze on all the accounts so no one could clean their information off the sites. Then all hell broke loose in that the police department got wind of the expanded investigation into all the social media sites. The FBI cyber unit was very busy as they were getting cyber information from some of the sites of some officers and command, including the chief.

This information was relayed to the governor, who was totally in shock. He immediately ordered the state police to suspend the police chief in question and take control of the department during the investigation. Upon the prearranged arrival of the state police, the police chief was waiting and ready to cooperate, telling them, "The governor was wrong to take this action as I have done nothing wrong." The state police also suspended a dozen other officers for their alleged involvement with antifa.

The governor knew this FBI case would take a while, so he temporarily assigned numerous state police to the police department for coverage. The FBI found a large cell of professional people such as lawyers, cops, doctors that were involved with this terror group. It was so unbelievable that this investigation made it to the president's desk. His attorney general had briefed the president on this case in full, and he would keep him updated as often as he had information. The investigation also revealed that large cash payments were being made into the account of antifa from some of the organizations the lawyers and doctors belonged to, as well as the police benevolent association (PBA).

The governor was so distressed with this news that he called the president and asked for the Department of Justice (DOJ) to step in due to their extended resources. After a few days, the president notified the DOJ of the police department investigation and the AG at the DOJ assigned ten investigators to the case and was confident they would find out what was going on. After a few weeks, the DOJ investigation revealed that there were many associated with antifa, and those names were given to the interim police chief. He in turn fired them all immediately for their affiliation with a known terror group. Some of them, after their firing, made threats that they would be seen again. The DOJ told the interim chief, "Threats were made, so be careful." It turned out that this scourge permeated all facets of our government and that it was so pervasive that the previous threats meant more now. The citizens were now questioning their own government. And it was hard to believe this started with a rock-and-roll club in south Florida.

There were numerous attempts by antifa in taking over police facilities and local businesses. The interim police chief was in a quandary, not knowing who was good and who was evil. He had gotten word that another rock-and-roll club was under siege by what they thought was antifa, or it could be a copycat. This was occurring in another nearby city. When the police responded to that club, they made numerous arrests, which included several ex-officers from the other police department. Those ex-officers had told their past chief that they would be back, and they were. The FBI responded to meet and interview those newly arrested, but they lawyered up very quickly so the FBI could not talk with them.

In a nearby van, the FBI discovered numerous pipe bombs, hand grenades, and several machine guns. They were planning an all-out assault either at the club or some government building like the police department or court. When the FBI evidence collection unit responded to remove the explosives, one of the techs mishandled one of the pipe bombs, causing it to explode, which in turn caused the many other explosives to detonate. Ammunition was going off along with several explosions. Tragically, several evidence technicians were killed instantly and many others seriously injured. The crime scene was huge as debris and bodies were scattered in all directions. This was a massive setback for the FBI as antifa cheered it.

Numerous other agents from other federal agencies responded as well as the local police departments. Antifa would now be the main target of the FBI and ATF. Word got to other club owners in the surrounding areas to be aware of any suspicious vehicles and people because of the explosive incident. Then in another part of town, a report came in that there was a massive car bomb that detonated at an African American club. There were mass casualties, so the FBI and ATF responded there. Luckily, there were only a few dozen people at the club, and the owner was one of the survivors. He told the FBI that was a large panel van parked next to the club in the parking lot, but no one gave it a second look.

The FBI was told that it was the van that exploded. The club owner was very distraught as his older brother and his brother's wife were among the dead. One side of the club was blown out as fires burned. The fire department and other officers arrived on scene as well as the medical examiner; it was a sad mess. The mayor held a press conference warning club owners that this retaliation was due to the many arrests that were made of the antifa group involving many police and state officials. He continued, telling the club owners, "Be vigilant and immediately report anything suspicious and hire security personnel if needed until we can end this terror streak."

Then later in the night while the clean-up was in progress, a warning from antifa was broadcast across all social media platforms, warning that a day of reckoning was coming and there would be a new world order and capitalism would be gone. The message was encrypted so it would be hard to trace the location of the transmission. The message was only a few seconds but scary and threatening. The FBI was aware of this domestic threat and quickly opened an investigation. All police departments were put on alert as well as the National Guard. The president was also looped in on this terror threat, and he told the FBI to work solely on this incident.

The original club owners are baffled as to how this spiraled out of control, stemming from their rock-and-roll club. The Black Lives Matter terror group had now joined antifa in destroying the fabric of our society. The FBI had a better handle on the BLM crowd and had undercover agents within that organization. Antifa had a large underground movement in recruiting new white guys who were losers in life, and there were plenty of them. Your background did not matter. There was a run on guns and ammo from the sporting goods stores in anticipation of massive trouble. The gun store owners loved it as their inventory was getting low and they did not care who bought as long they passed the background check by the state and feds.

The ATF was worried as to the amount of guns and ammo that was being sold and to whom. But they had no control over who bought as long as they had a clean background check. The feds knew from past experiences that many with a clean background check commit heinous crimes. They had a good feeling that some of the guns sold would be found in the hands of antifa and BLM. Then some devastating news:

there was a massive prison break and several of the high-ranking antifa were some that escaped. They were heard telling others that if they got out, they would rejoin their other antifa friends and really cause havoc.

Now all the police and federal authorities were on alert for potential trouble as the federal marshals were looking to recapture the escapees. The word got out to the media about the possible trouble brewing and about the escape. This now panicked the community, who went through a riot and destruction and now feared it would happen again, so again they boarded up their businesses and hired many armed security guards. The governor had put the National Guard on standby as a precaution. The FBI now looked to interview the past club owners to see if they had any dealings with any anti-American people, for any clues that might have been missed.

But after the interviews, there was no new information obtained. Reports were now coming in that there were several break-ins of gun stores and several carjackings near the prison. The FBI and local police believed that this was done by the escapees and that they might be plotting some type of an attack. The FBI intelligence and the NSA were picking up chatter from several radical groups that kept mentioning the names of the escapees. They still could not be located, but the FBI was getting close. The FBI was then notified that an escapee was found in an apartment, overdosed on heroin. The FBI and the local homicide unit arrived and sealed the apartment, as this would hopefully lead to the other escapees and their plight.

Then in an adjacent apartment, two more bodies were discovered, both dead by overdose; this time it was another escapee and an unknown female, both found with the syringe in an arm. These two had keys to the carjacked vehicles as well as numerous firearms in a duffel bag, probably stolen from the gun store. This was good news to the FBI, but there were still a few guys missing. Then the FBI was notified that the remaining escapees had turned themselves in to the police station and were being held there, and now this accounted for all the escapees. Eventually, the surviving escapees spoke with the FBI and told them that their friends were to meet up with other antifa members and go on a destructive rampage killing as many cops as they could before possible being killed themselves.

Then ATF arrived and took possession of the stolen guns but then discovered that there were still many firearms missing, and they were desperate to find out where they were. So the ATF agents went to the police station to interrogate the two escapees. Upon entering the police station, they heard a loud commotion and ran toward the holding area inside. They saw one of the escapees lying in a pool of blood after apparently being attacked by a police officer. Unfortunately, the suspect died from his wounds, and the officer was taken into custody. The remaining escapee was removed and placed into protective custody. The ATF agents then lost it with the officer telling him, "These two have information on the remaining stolen guns that are out in the neighborhood and now this is in the shit."

The officer told the ATF agents, "These antifa scumbags killed my brother at a political rally, and I just lost it."

The ATF agent told the officer, "You sure did. Now you're going to jail for murder."

The officer said, "That's OK. I got revenge for my brother." The officer was removed and turned over to the homicide detective and Internal Affairs. The officer was interrogated and booked into the jail under a murder charge.

The remaining escapee now refused to talk after seeing his buddy beaten to death, so the ATF talked with their boss and were able to make a deal for information. If the suspect revealed the whereabouts of the remaining stolen guns, he would be transferred to a medium-custody prison closer to his family, and he took the deal. He told the ATF agents that they were to pick up the guns at a friend's home just outside the city.

The suspect supplied the address, and the ATF agents went to their office and got with their SWAT team as they waited for a search warrant. The warrant was obtained, and the SWAT team went to the house. The house looked very nice: two stories, brick, nice landscaping, and a large fountain in front with a winding driveway. Several local officers also on the scene went to the adjacent homes and had them leave for their own safety until the SWAT operation was over. The team moved to the front door, knocked, and announced, "Federal agents, search warrant." They were then met with a barrage of gunfire from the windows and through the front door, hitting several agents.

Luckily, their injuries were not life-threatening. The agents backed out as they did not have a target and there might be kids inside, so they took cover and called for a negotiator. While waiting for the negotiator, the local police were locking down the area and evacuating the nearby homes. When the negotiator got on scene, he gathered information on the shooter, and when he ascertained the suspect's name, he believed he had heard it before but did not know from where. The negotiator asks around to several of the police officers and with the fire personnel. When the fire personnel heard the name, they were floored; the name they were told was one of the new owners of the rock-and-roll club that was burned down by antifa.

Word spread very quickly on who the shooter was, and no one could believe it. This information was given to the negotiator, who quickly got a rapport going with the shooter. The negotiator was told by the shooter that he was tired of fighting with this group, so he felt he had to join them even after what they did to his business and friends. The police and negotiator had a hard time coming to grips with this fireman that crossed the line.

After approximately several hours and trying to get him to come out unarmed, it was learned that his wife and kids were being held in an undisclosed area and that he had to sacrifice himself to keep his family alive. The suspect was told by the members of antifa that if he wanted to keep his family alive, he had to attack the police in a murderous assault and to be prepared to die for the cause.

The shooter had to make a decision to give up and possibly have his family killed or take one for the team and come out shooting. The suspect really did not want to die, but he could not let his family and young kids die. He called the group holding his family and told them he would sacrifice himself, so the group told him where the family could be located. The suspect told the captors, "Once my family was safe, I would come out shooting." The group let the family go and gave the location to the suspect fireman, who in turn gave that information to the police negotiator. He then sent a team to the area to find the family and they did, and they were unharmed. The negotiator obtained the information on the family, who in turn told the suspect.

He was glad his family was safe and then made good on his decision. Windows were now being broken as the shooter came out armed. He started screaming and then pointed his gun in the direction of the police, at which time they open fire, killing the suspect. The on-scene firefighters were crying and in disbelief as they did not know the back story about the fireman's family. They started to wonder how a decorated fireman, business owner, and family man went so astray—so many questions and very few answers. News then traveled fast, and the FBI picked up chatter on the radio that the antifa members were celebrating the death of the fireman and what they achieved. But this case and investigation were not over.

The FBI had many leads they were following, and they were from all over the country. One lead that most interested them was a conversation that involved a takeover and shutdown of an airport, and not just any airport but the airport in Atlanta, Georgia, the busiest in the country. The FBI in Atlanta were notified as well as the Atlanta police stationed at the airport. The only issue was when this might occur. Antifa members would possibly be dressed as normal traveling passengers and not in their black garb. Days went by without any incidents until there was a disturbance on a plane, which got the attention of the Atlanta police, at which time dozens of young men and women broke through a security door and rushed onto the tarmac, blocking planes at the gate and on the runway. This caught the police off guard and caused many delays for the traveling public, and of course, this caused a ripple effect across the country. Numerous police officers responded along with the FBI.

While on the runway, the terrorists broke bottles and other debris in the path of the planes, hoping to get some flat tires. They had signs praising the fallen fireman who helped them and other signs saying, "Death to America" and "America is no more." Now the riot squad and SWAT were on scene and started to arrest the thugs on federal charges as well as state charges. But these assholes did not want to go quietly, they fought during the arrest resulting in many having to go to the hospital as well as a dentist.

CHAPTER 12

No law enforcement were injured, and they had the backing of their administration to take care of business. After approximately two hours, the thugs were removed and arrested and taken to the jail in the airport for processing and then to the federal building to see the federal magistrate, to face their federal charges.

All were held without bond on terroristic charges. Word got out about the group being arrested, which filtered to other gang members as well as BLM. The anarchists gathered around the police station and started throwing rocks and pointing lasers at the responding officers. The group had grown very quickly and supported by others from the neighborhood just out looking for trouble. The violent crowd grew very quickly and got more vocal and violent. Many fights broke out between people in the crowd as the police stood by and watched. The Molotov cocktails were being thrown, and now the police would take action. They summoned their water cannon and aimed it at the larger group of protesters.

The order was given to turn on the cannon, and with a massive amount of power and force, the water came out and took out the crowds very quickly. Many protesters were thrown several hundred feet from the water pressure. This did the trick and much of the crowd cleared out and things calmed down. There were a few minor injuries, but that's life. Because of all the violence outside the police station, the FBI decided to make a grand exit via helicopter. They called for their bird, and it landed on the landing pad on top of the police station. It would have to make several trips due to the capacity on board. But it was a safer way to go so each flight carried eight suspects plus the FBI. It took eight trips for all to be removed from the station.

As all the mayhem was appearing to calm down, numerous flights were coming in from areas where the antifa was a big problem. After several of the planes had landed and emptied, the cleaning crews came in to clean the planes and found booklets from antifa on how to shut down a city and take control. Some of the cleaning crews gave this booklet to the airport security, who in turn turned it over to the FBI. It appeared that there might be an upcoming event where destruction and shutdowns might occur from antifa. Some of the local nightlife clubs were on alert for any potential problems from this group. Then one of the bouncers noticed a jacket one of the club patrons was wearing and knew it was the antifa symbol. This bouncer got with his boss, who in turn called the police. The police detained this suspect and then called out the FBI.

The suspect was very enraged about being detained, feeling that he did nothing wrong. Threats were being made toward the club personnel and police. Upon arrival of the FBI, they took the suspect into custody for questioning and removed him to their headquarters. Upon arrival at the FBI, they were met by numerous others shouting to release their friend. During the FBI interview, the suspect had told them that he flew in from Portland because he and others were thinking of opening a rock-and-roll club in the area after they heard about a club in South Florida called The Hurt.

The FBI asked the suspect if he knew what happened to that club, and his reply was "Yeah. But they fucked it up. I know how to work a club without any problems or criminal activity."

The FBI had a feeling that this guy might want to open this club to recruit new members, but they could not be sure. Anyone from Portland was a suspect agitator and possible member of antifa. But at this time, the FBI had nothing on these guys. The Portland group got all their ducks in a row to get a large bank loan to start their new venture of a nice rock-and-roll club. But they ran into many hurdles after they were approved for a loan.

They had to go before the city commission and get variances for their building plus hear from the public since the last debacle. At several commission meetings, the public spoke and did not like the idea of a new club because of what had happened in the past and all the violence it created, but then there were those who felt that a new beginning was needed for the city and that it would create jobs and entertainment for the approved area. It would now be a few months before they heard anything, just enough time for the feds to check into the group. But it appeared that these guys had flown under the radar and seemed clean. But were they?

By now, most of the disturbances were quelled by the city, with many arrests made. The jails were filled but most bonded out on misdemeanor charges. But many others remained in jail pending felony charges. There were even some prominent politicians posting bail for the arrestees. These were the anti-police and defund-the-police crowd.

Many were suspicious about this group wanting to build a new club. They had a feeling it would be déjà vu, and they did not want to see that again. But at this time, there was no legal reason to not permit them to build the club. Once this group got all their permits and licenses, the FBI infiltrated the construction company to keep a close eye on things.

Meanwhile back in Portland, the antifa thugs were busy getting new recruits, mainly rich white kids, and they were going to Florida and getting on the construction site as workers and awaiting further orders from their leaders. This got back to the FBI that was working as part of the club construction company, and all they could to was to watch and wait. As time marched on, week after week, there were no problems or issues with the work crews. So the FBI brass decided to remove their undercovers from the construction site, but it did not go unnoticed by a few. They did keep a distant eye on the building company. But just like the FBI thought, the new construction employees were funneling in small weapons like firearms and dynamite.

They were building secret compartments to store the weapons until they were needed, and only a very few would know where they were hidden. Months passed and the club was near completion and it was being billed as a very exclusive, expensive, and private club for the elite, politicians, and the rich. The management were hiring very beautiful females and very handsome men, which would help bring in business. The club advertised everywhere: Internet, TV, radio, and movie theaters. They were selling memberships starting at $500 for the year and up to $1,500 for the big VIPs. So they knew that the clientele would be upscale, keeping the garbage out. There were many in the area that had money and did not mind spending it on something special.

They sold out of all their initial memberships, approximately 800. Now it was getting close to opening day as the staff was hired: chefs, security (big muscle-heads), and valet parking company. The management also hired several off-duty police officers to be on the property and they would be in uniform. The female staff wore a very revealing uniform that had the club logo along with their name embroidered on it. Most of the female were large breasted, which was a big help in bringing in clients with a lot of cash. There were also several very private rooms with locking doors just in case the client wanted some private time with one of the girls, but it was very costly.

The police were given posters of several antifa members to be posted in the area just in case. Two of the kitchen help were on those posters, so they had to quickly and quietly quit and get out. These two thugs contacted their handler and told them about the posters, so the handler sent in two others that were not on any poster and living in the shadows. The two new members were believed to be very radical and without any criminal records. These two had their hands in bombings, arson, shootings, and physical violence, and they were not afraid of anything. But they always escaped justice somehow. The FBI was made aware of these two and was able to get their pedigree and could find nothing in their backgrounds.

A deeper investigation revealed that they had a very good and faithful friend in the Portland PD, a senior police officer. The FBI contacted their people in Portland, who in turn brought in this officer for questioning. They got a subpoena and checked this officer's financials and discovered that large sums of money were deposited after each violent attack by these two antifa thugs in Florida. This officer was their protection, which is why the two thugs did not have a record;

they were protected by the officer. Upon interrogation and the threat of many years in federal prison, he confessed. He told the FBI that he was friends with the antifa thugs and took care of them if they were arrested at a riot. The officer would take custody of them and then release them blocks from the crime scenes.

Then a large sum of money was transferred into an obscure account. The FBI contacted the police chief and brought him up to speed on the investigation. The senior officer was immediately fired, and the FBI interrogation continued. After the interrogation, the officer was arrested and booked into the county jail. Now the FBI in Florida could intervene and arrest the two new thugs at the club. The local sheriff's office and FBI SWAT team went to the club and found the two new antifa members in the kitchen and arrested them without incident. The two were taken into custody and held in the local jail, pending extradition. Approximately a week later, the judge granted the extradition warrant, and both were taken back to Portland to stand trial.

Meanwhile, the club was open and operating without incident but under a close eye of the feds. The club was packed every night with local politicians and local celebrities. The girls were making a lot of money, and the private locked rooms were occupied each night. The mayor of the city was told about the private locked rooms and felt that there was prostitution going on, so he ordered the police department to go undercover and find out. So one night, several undercover detectives dressed nice and showed off their jewelry and flashed a roll of cash.

They worked the room, showing off, and were able to connect with several of the girls working. They were able to get into the private room and almost immediately were approached for cash for sex.

They made a deal and then identified themselves as police detectives and arrested the girls. The girls were removed from the club uncuffed so as to not cause an incident. The girls were taken out the back of the club to a waiting police car to be brought to the station for processing. Upon arrival at the police station, they were met by the FBI. They wanted information on the club and its activity. The girls were told that if they cooperated, no charges would be brought against them. They both agreed as they would not do well in jail. They would wear a hidden camera and record dealings with the owners and staff.

After several weeks, the only information obtained was of several patrons snorting cocaine, but then a video showed the mayor trying to pick up a girl after it was him who asked the police chief to set up something. The mayor was also seen cozying up to the new employees from Portland. At this time, the FBI had no criminal issues. But as time went by, suspicious activity was taking place such as after-hours late-night male visitors and truck shipments into the morning hours. This information got back to the FBI, who then set up on the club, videotaping any and all after-hours activity.

They then followed one of the subjects who left the area by car and carrying a large garbage bag to the city dump. This guy dumped the bag in a large pile and departed. The FBI then retrieved the garbage bag to check it. They took the bag to their office, and what they discovered was shocking to them and a potential criminal case. In the bag were several notebooks with large payments for guns, drugs, and money to pay for antifa recruitments. There was also a list of names from years ago when the first Hurt club was opened. Names like Bob, Glenn, Josh, and Russ showed that they too had ties to antifa. The notes showed that these individuals were a recruitment team unknown to many, seeking out possible members and acting like a sleeper cell for terrorists. But unfortunately, or fortunately, for them, they died for the cause. Why these notebooks were thrown away after all this time was something the FBI would have to look into. And were the new management of the club plotting something?

The FBI had to backtrack into the lives of those that worked at the old club before and then work forward again, hoping to link everyone. Meanwhile, the BLM group was forging ahead with their destructive plans since all the attention was on the antifa. The BLM thugs felt emboldened since the FBI was too busy with antifa, so they were able to wiggle their way into the new rock club, posing as high rollers with a lot of cash to blow. A few months went by without incident, and negotiations started to transfer the club ownership to the BLM. The owners felt too much heat from the feds, so they wanted out before they got arrested and jailed. So eventually the club was sold to members of the BLM, and the old owners went back to Portland.

When the old owners got back to their home base in Portland, their handlers were not pleased that they blew their terroristic plans. Then one night, joggers in a park found several bodies dead on the grass, apparently from gunshot wounds. The bosses did not like that the two old club owners failed them, possibly bringing heat upon them. Soon the FBI learned of the homicides and traveled to Portland to work the investigation with the Portland police. The homicides were relayed to the South Florida law enforcement, so they kept a close eye on those running the club. The Hurt now had a very bad reputation for its affiliation with known thugs aka BLM, so the city commission started to work on shutting it down.

This information got back to the club management, so they decided to do what they did best, burn it down with people in it. So one night when there were plenty of patrons, including some city officials and police, they blocked some of the exits and started a fire as they ran out and disappeared into the night. The fire spread very rapidly, trapping many inside, but luckily, most got out. Several commissioners and female waitstaff were the ones trapped. As the fire kept growing, the fire department arrived and it took them almost four hours to get the fire under control.

Sadly, as the fire was knocked down, they made their way inside and found many bodies trapped behind blocked or locked doors. Most seemingly died from smoke inhalation while others were badly burned. This was a mass-casualty, mass-homicide scene caused by the BLM thugs. The city gathered the remaining commissioners for an emergency meeting along with the police chief, FBI, and ATF. They needed to get to the bottom of this horrific tragedy and find those responsible and bring them to justice quickly. They also pledged that moving forward, there would be no more rock-and-roll clubs built in the city limits because of all the problems they attracted.

The FBI acted quickly, and with numerous leads and witness accounts, they tracked down the BLM culprits with the help of the US Marshals. The BLM thugs were tracked back to Portland. The three possibly involved in the arson/homicides were scatted throughout the city. Two were taken into custody as they were having lunch at a restaurant. The third refused to be arrested and barricaded himself in his home on the outskirts of the city. The FBI SWAT team was called in along with a negotiator. The local police had to evacuate the nearby homes as a perimeter was established. The negotiator was on the phone for hours with the suspect but to no avail.

He was not coming out and yelling out the window, "I'm not going to jail." Then the SWAT team shot several rounds of tear gas into the home and unfortunately started a fire. Then the negotiator attempted another phone call but no answer. The front door of the home burst open, and the suspect came out, firing an AK-47 at the SWAT team. Several SWAT members returned fire, killing the suspect; no officers were injured. The SWAT team then entered the home for clearance and discovered the suspect's wife dead in the bedroom from a gunshot wound to the head. The home was filled with hate posters wanting cops dead, encouraging riots and looting and hatred of white people. The scene was secured, and the FBI's evidence recovery team moved in to do their job.

After many hours, the bodies were removed and taken to the medical examiner for autopsy. The other evidence was taken and would be used in the trials of the other BLM members. The two other suspects were arraigned and given no bail. But surprisingly, several high-profile black politicians in DC put up their money for lawyers for the two suspects. It was obvious that these politicians had a hatred for the cops, no sympathy for those killed in the arson, and a hatred for the country. The two suspects were denied bond and sat in federal custody for many months until their trials. The US attorney's office had plenty of evidence to convict the suspects, and when the trials started, the jury was quick to convict on all criminal counts.

Several months later at the sentencing, they were given life in prison without parole. The gallery in the courtroom was not happy with the sentence and started to threaten the attorney and judge. Those protesting were friends of the suspects and probable BLM members. They were removed from the courtroom and then spread the word via text messages about the sentences, resulting in large pro-BLM crowds showing up at the courthouse in numbers. Now because of the quickly organized protests, the local police and sheriff's office had to respond in their riot gear. After the court case was completed, the attorneys and judge had to be escorted to their cars in the garage to get out safely. But the crowd outside was hell-bent on destruction.

They started throwing rocks and bottles at the police and building. Several cars were set on fire and then of course antifa showed up and added to the mayhem. They attempted to start fights with the police, but then a new group was seen entering the fracas. A group called the Proud Boys, which did not like the two other groups, showed up. This group was all white men with a racist history. They showed up en masse and very quickly as word spread of the confrontation. These guys carried knives, guns, and clubs and were not afraid to use them. Then more police reinforcements showed up and with a water cannon. The cannon shot high-pressure water at the groups and forced them to the ground and dispersed them. The police helicopter hovering over the riot communicated to the ground troops that some of the crowd was moving to a different location and for police units to move there also.

Then shots rang out from the crowd as many tried to run. The police were not sure at first where the shots came from. As the crowd thinned, police observed several rioters on the ground with fatal gunshot wounds. Because of the crowd size, it took paramedics longer to respond, and they were not going to come into an unsafe scene. Then a short distance away, several fights between the Proud Boys and BLM broke out. A Proud Boy member was being detained as he was the one with the firearm. Riot police responded and took the shooter into custody. Then this guy was yelling that it was self-defense as the people attacked him from the crowd. The gun was recovered, and the suspect was removed and taken to the police station.

But then several of the Proud Boys went to the police station to start mayhem; they were upset that their friend was arrested for defending himself. Then the few became many and surrounded the police station, trapping those inside. They were chanting, "Let him out, let him out." Several in the crowd started to throw bottles at the police building, along with rocks, breaking windows. Then the police command called for the water cannon to be brought to the police station to remove the crowds from the front of the building.

The cannon responded and removed many from the front of the building. The detectives were then able to remove their suspect and take him to the jail.

A police car pulled up to the front and received the prisoner for transport to jail. As the vehicle departed, it was met with rocks, resulting in the car receiving several broken windows. The police car attempted to get out of the area fast, but with broken windows and glass on the officers, it was difficult driving. The car eventually crashed into a light police, totaling the car and injuring the officers. Then a few of the Proud Boys got to the car and released their friend, who was handcuffed, and escaped with him. A few moments later, the officers came to and discovered their prisoner was missing. They radioed in, resulting in the beginning of a manhunt. K-9s, a helicopter, and the US Marshals responded to aid in the search.

The suspect had a good hour head start before police resources were able to start their track. But what was equally bad was that the suspect was able to grab his gun back that the officers had in the car and were transporting to the evidence rom. The police were quick to arrest those who threw the rocks earlier at the police car, and they would face felony charges for aiding in the escape. They were quickly arraigned and given no bond and then removed to jail. Word of the turmoil spread overseas to Europe. Antifa and BLM joined forces and traveled to the United States and then traveled to Portland to meet up with the leaders of those two terror groups. They were formulating a plan on a very large scale to fight the government in all areas as well as causing havoc within communities.

These groups were very secretive about the meetings, keeping the police in the dark, hoping to get the jump on them. They were getting very well organized and started to travel throughout the country, including DC. They started to stockpile weapons and bomb-making materials. Several of those that came to the United States were bomb makers in their countries. After several weeks, things had calmed down to the point where the police were a little laid back and, for once, not thinking about the terror groups. But unbeknownst to them, there was a war brewing between the antifa, BLM, and the law enforcement community. Small skirmishes started to break out between the police and the terror groups to see how the police would respond. The police had a limited response to quell the disturbance.

A BLM member started to make notes of the police roll calls and of how many would be on the road during a roll call. They were formulating a plan to block off the police parking lots, keeping most of the officers inside and blocked in. If they were able to keep most of the officers from any response, it would be a victory and give them an advantage in property destruction. This BLM member went back to his handlers with the surveillance information for them to contemplate and possibly act on.

Then the leaders of the two terror groups decided that their first targets would be the rock-and-roll clubs since this was where most of the problems started. There were several in and around the Portland area.

Their plan was a violent one. They were to enter the clubs with hidden explosives, which would be set off remotely, and anyone trying to leave would be shot down from outside. This was going to be a bloodbath. They would pick a busy weekend night when the clubs were packed. They knew that they would be the first group looked at by law enforcement. So they had to be quick and then disappear. There would be simultaneous attacks throughout the country: New York, Fort Lauderdale, Atlanta, and Los Angeles. The terror groups would contain the police inside their police stations and surveil those driving around to get a feel of how many officers would be on the road at one time.

The group's leaders were waiting for all their intel to come back to them before they made a decision on when to act and when they would get maximum destruction. Many members were already in their target cities and had brought their weapons into the clubs already and were acting as sleeper terrorist cells. The leaders decided to act on a holiday weekend coming up soon, thinking that the clubs would be very busy. To their knowledge, no law enforcement had any knowledge of the upcoming plot. Many of the terror members had rented RVs to store much of their explosives and purchased a message amplifier system to relay messages for anyone in the area to get out and give a fifteen-minute countdown.

The message would say "remove yourselves from the area immediately, you have fifteen minutes," and each minute, it would give the same warning. The word was handed down from the leaders that this upcoming weekend would be the target date for their message to the world in response to the killing of unarmed black men and the capitalistic society. The target weekend was here, and the RVs were placed close to the rock-and-roll clubs. At approximately 11:00 p.m., the messages were being played very loudly, and at first, those walking nearby thought it was a message from the clubs. But then some thought to get out as the threats might be true. Several law enforcement personnel arrived at the clubs after concerned people called 911 about the threat messages.

Then the countdown was at one when two officers peered into the RV. Then it happened, a massive explosion instantly killing the two officers and destroying the club and many surrounding buildings. Numerous people were killed that were at the front of the club. Others started to escape from the ruins and were immediately gunned down by several of the surviving antifa and BLM members who had been in a safe place inside the club. This was taking place at the same time in the other target cities. Their plans were working and locking in the police at their police stations was also working but only for a while. As the officers started to emerge from their building, they were met with gunfire, at which time they returned fire, killing everyone that was firing at them.

They then were able to get out and respond to the bombing scenes. Many dead terrorists lay near the police stations, resulting in major crime scenes, which brought in the FBI and ATF. This was an unprecedented attack on American innocence. The president was briefed on the attacks and pledged the full support of the federal government. Unfortunately, the fire department and paramedics could not get close to the scene because of the possibility that there were still other terrorists with weapons. Numerous SWAT teams arrived and started to clear the scenes and found no other threats at each target city. It would take days for the crime scenes to be cleared and the areas opened to the public. By the end of the horrific attacks, there were 40 dead terrorists and 120 dead club patrons.

There were no words to describe all the carnage. The president decided to go on TV and speak about the attacks and told the American people that all would be done to bring to justice those behind the attacks and the government would pay for the funeral expenses. The DOJ started the investigation, which sent them overseas to Europe, where the terror thugs came from. The DOJ opened a very wide-ranging investigation, which included looking into many prominent members of police departments and state attorneys' offices. The president said anyone and everyone was fair game. The president unleashed hell on those believed to be members of the two terror organizations.

There was an all-out assault on the antifa and BLM groups, and it was not pretty—hundreds of search warrants, subpoenas and arrests on the federal level. Most of this went on with little to no problem, but a few decided to put up a fight and lost. The Department of Homeland Security put extra Customs inspectors at any airport where they took in international flights. The highest scrutiny was established to prevent anyone that might have affiliations with any terror groups from coming into the States. This program was working very well; the feds turned away many that were suspicious, with possible terror ties. Meanwhile, all the crime scene units at the rock-and-roll clubs that were targeted had finished; many unexploded bombs and firearms were recovered and taken into property.

They would be examined by the ATF and FBI crime labs to determine who obtained them and where they came from. Then they would see how much the investigation will expand and who might be arrested. A public information officer (PIO) from the FBI gave a news conference and spoke about the investigation and what they had found so far, to be as transparent as possible. The mainstream media in usual fashion asked the most ridiculous questions as the conservative media asked pointed questions. The mainstream media were asking gotcha questions, but the FBI PIO would have none of that. He was so pissed off with them that he ended the press conference early and stormed off. The FBI director was not too thrilled with his PIOs performance but let it go.

Around the country, federal courts were hearing the cases against the terror groups under heavy security. US Marshals had security on the perimeter of the courthouse, and the court security was beefed up inside. They could not keep out the audience for the trials, which consisted of members of the groups on trial. The judges had their own personal security. The defendants on trial were nasty and threatening to the judge and prosecutor. During the trials, the defendants were very disruptive and threatening to the witnesses. At the Florida trials, the defendants kept on yelling out the names of their friends killed by the police, names like Bob, Russ, and many others.

The judges ordered the defendants to keep quiet, and if not, they would be gagged during the trial. After approximately ten minutes, several of the defendants again disrupted the proceedings, and thus, the judge ordered the defendants gagged. Then one of the court officers approached the judge with a note given to him by a stranger. The note was a bomb threat to the building. The judge made an announcement that there was a bomb threat and that the court was adjourned until further notice. The jury and attorneys were taken out the back and the defendants, who were smiling, were removed back to their cells in the basement of the building.

Many others were told to leave until the building was searched by the bomb squad. Upon their arrival, they deployed their bomb dogs and started the search. After approximately one hour, one of the dogs alerted them to a suspicious package that was taped under the judge's desk. They then deployed their bomb robot in an attempt to remove the suspect device. The package was removed very slowly as the bomb squad watched on a closed-circuit TV from the mounted camera on the robot. As soon as the robot started to move away from the judge's desk with the device, it went off, a very loud explosion and fireball. Luckily, no one was hurt, and the damage was fairly minimal. Now this trial would be delayed for a short time as the FBI and ATF investigated. They would collect all the physical evidence, any videos from the courthouse cameras, and any possible eyewitnesses.

The only people that were allowed into the courtroom before the trial were bailiffs, clerks, and law enforcement. The FBI obtained video from the courtroom and observed only two people that were behind the judge's desk: a clerk and a bailiff. A closer look then showed the female clerk get down low out of camera view behind the desk, but she was not carrying anything in her hands. Whatever she possibly had was hidden under her clothes. The FBI found her and brought her in for questioning. As she sat in the FBI office, they noticed that she had a small tattoo on her upper arm. It said "ANT/BLM lives." As the questioning was about to begin, the clerk yelled out, "I want a lawyer." Now all questioning had to stop until she was represented by a lawyer.

Meanwhile, the FBI got a search warrant for her apartment. During the search, they found a lot of pro-antifa and BLM materials. They also found bomb-making materials. The FBI felt that the clerk did not make the bomb but was there when it was made, and she knew who made it. Then one of the crime scene techs found a pin-on button that said "Juror" on it. Could one of the jury members be the bomb maker? The FBI immediately responded back to the courthouse to meet with a bailiff who handed out those buttons. Upon contact with him, they asked if any juror was given a second button. The bailiff said yes and who it was; he told them the name. The FBI then tracked down that juror and brought him in for questioning.

The juror had an idea why he was there and told the FBI he wanted a lawyer. So again they could not ask any questions but then obtained a search warrant for his home. This juror was a married man with two young kids. When the FBI responded to the juror's home, they were greeted by the wife. She was handed a copy of the search warrant, and the crime techs went in. They immediately confiscated the computers and several cellphones. They then entered a locked room, and upon entering, they found bomb materials and books on how to make a bomb. The FBI then went back and placed the juror under arrest.

After the FBI placed the juror under arrest, they left him in the interrogation room. He apparently was not searched, and when the

FBI left the room, the juror took out a small knife and cut his throat. He bled out pretty quick. When the FBI agents returned to the room, they found the juror on the floor, bleeding from the neck wound. They quickly attempted first aid, but it was too late; the juror was dead. Now the FBI agents had a lot of explaining to do to their bosses. This was a very unfortunate situation, losing their bombing suspect. But they had the bomber's notebook, which had many names and phone numbers of possible co-conspirators.

Then the FBI was notified of other bomb threats against federal facilities, and when those buildings were searched, nothing was found, to their surprise. Also receiving threats were several of the large airports, in an attempt to slow down air travel. There were many airlines that had to evacuate the planes and terminals and then had to re-screen everyone. The airport police and federal agents at the airports helped with the search, which was a massive undertaking. The roads leading into the airports had to be shut down to limit the number of the cars at the terminals. Several aviation units also helped with the search from the air. Nothing suspicious was discovered, and the searches did not turn up anything, just more threats at this time.

So the scenes were cleared and traffic allowed back into the airports. The delays were nationwide as well as spreading to other countries. Now the FBI was attempting to track down those responsible for the threats. The FBI investigation took them to Europe and into the heart of London. London had a large problem with antifa just like the United States was having. Interpol also assisted with the investigation. London had splinter groups of antifa throughout London, and after Interpol got involved, they tracked down a group that worked from a rock-and-roll club in downtown London. For whatever reason, antifa liked using rock-and-roll clubs as a backdrop for their criminality.

The London police along with the FBI raided the club and detained several antifa members just as they were attempting to hack into the US air traffic control system at a Washington DC airport as well as Joint Base Andrews. The timing could not be better because if they were to hack into the air traffic control at Joint Base Andrews, it would have been a disaster for the military and the president on Air Force One. The antifa thugs were taken into custody and interrogated by the London police and FBI. The FBI discovered that one of the antifa members was communicating with a US airman in the tower at Joint Base Andrews. The FBI in London immediately contacted their office in DC, and they sent several special agents to meet with the US airman at the airport.

The FBI arrived at the airport and immediately detained the airman and took him to their office for an interview. They also confiscated his cellphone and laptop computer. The FBI read the airman his Miranda warnings, at which time the airman said he wanted a lawyer, at which time the FBI could not question him. So the FBI arrested the airman on conspiracy charges and took him to jail. The federal judge denied bail and the airman stayed in custody pending the trial. The US attorney was contacted by the defense attorney that was assigned by the government. He wanted to meet to mitigate any jail time his client might have to serve, in exchange for information on other ongoing criminal acts by the local antifa group.

But what the FBI and TSA missed was all the young people coming into the States from Europe. There was one flight attendant that thought about that on one flight, but no one else thought about it. What they did not know was that those young people (twenty to thirty years old) were antifa members coming to make trouble and to back up their other members stateside. There were many hundreds of them on many different flights from London, Australia, France, and Italy. On the planes, they were talking about sightseeing in NY and Washington DC. Upon their arrival, they spread out between the two cities and met up with their counterparts. In the coming days, the president of the United States was to make a speech about lawlessness in politics.

He put out a tweet that on a certain date, they would come to the DC area for the speech; this information also went out to the antifa in NYC. Back in DC, the mayor issued a permit for a protest the day of the speech and alerted her police department as well as Homeland Security. Many of the rock-and-roll clubs owned by the antifa were to shut down to attend the protest, which was supposed to be peaceful. The antifa mob put out a statement to their members: "Dress as if you support the president, then we will attack," the old Trojan horse tactic.

Then the day of the speech, many supporters of the president started to show up. The police had barricades set up, which were working fine.

There was a stage for the president and large speakers. There were a few speeches prior, then the president. The president stirred up the crowd and pointed to the Capitol building and said, "There is our problem." The crowd cheered and stayed very peaceful. When the president finished, he departed back to the White House. By this time, the crowd was very large, probably close to 100,000 and still very peaceful—many flags, banners, and chanting. What the mayor did not anticipate was the tens of thousands that that showed up, outnumbering the police 100 to 1. But then like turning on a light switch, the crowd charged at the police and attempted to jump the barricades and attacked law enforcement.

Just the sheer number of suspects pushing their way past the police was crazy. Many officers were hurt; pepper spray was in the air and riot batons swinging. A call was placed by the police chief for more help and it was on the way but not soon enough. The mob was able to get to the Capitol building where many scaled the walls, broke windows and gained entry into some of the chambers. People were heard yelling "burn it down, burn it down" then another loud voice from the end of the hall: "We got him, we got him." A congressman was cornered and had his hand tied with zip ties from one of the rioters. A large crowd gathered around the congressman; he was taunted as he screamed to be released. He was then dragged off to a small room and held there by his captors. Meanwhile, there were many Congress people and their staff inside sheltering in place until they could be escorted out. Tear gas was permeating through the air, so the congressmen and women were told to use their gas masks. When it was safe, the Capitol police escorted everyone to safety without incident.

Certain protective rooms had their windows broken out as the protesters attempted entry. At one point, a woman was able to get in and was shot and killed by the Capitol police. Word spread quickly about an active shooter, which was false. Many of the protesters got into many offices of the government leaders and had pictures taken of them by friends. Of course, the national media immediately put out the narrative that the president's supporters were the culprits without any evidence as usual. Many still photos of the mob inside showed them with antifa tattoos on their arms and hands, proving their Trojan horse attack. Then many SWAT teams made their way through the building, clearing out everyone and making scores of arrests.

Approximately four hours later, all clear was given for Congress to continue. Outside the Capitol, calm was being restored with many more arrests for curfew violations and weapons possession. It was only now that news spread of the kidnapping of a congressman and where he was being held. The news spread pretty quickly to the federal law enforcement. Several SWAT teams made their way inside and to the room where the congressman was being held. It was also learned that there were three others in the room, also probably antifa. A negotiator was called in to get the congressman out safely. The congressman was yelling to get him out and that the suspects were armed with knives.

CHAPTER 13

After approximately one hour, two of the suspects gave up and came out quietly as the third was refusing and threatening to kill the congressman. After about an hour, a gunshot was heard, and the SWAT team broke down the door and found the third suspect dead from a sniper's bullet. The congressman was not hurt. He was freed from the zip ties and escorted out to an ambulance to be checked out. He was fine but shaken up. The dead suspect was a diehard antifa member. The surviving two suspects were taken into custody by the FBI and held for interrogation. Sweeps were then being done at the DNC and RNC, where they discovered pipe bombs and gasoline.

They were removed by the bomb squad without incident. The president then came on TV and condemned the violence and the attacks on the police and said he felt bad about the death that occurred. But it looked like antifa had won its battle. The president was now taking a beating over the violence that he did not commit or instigate. Many close to the president are distancing themselves from him, even those who had always supported him. Then information surfaced that several Democratic members may have also been involved in the Capitol riot and may have been hoping that the president would take the fall.

Antifa all over the country and Europe were rejoicing after their efforts paid off. But they continued to cause problems at many other state houses and courthouses by protesting in front of those places and fighting with the police. Although no one was badly injured, there was a lot of damage to vehicles and buildings. Some of the rock-and-roll clubs had antifa nights where the terror mobs congratulated each other over their destruction and win. But they were not going to celebrate for long.

The Secret Service, FBI, and Homeland Security had a trove of evidence and video of those that caused havoc. They used facial recognition and identified many suspects. The feds spread out with the help of the US Marshals service and rounded up many of the antifa suspects. Back in DC, the Congress was in session, and they debated if they should invoke the Twenty-fifth Amendment to remove the president or to just impeach him again. This sounded like a good idea, but this president had only a few weeks left in office and there would not be time to impeach, and the vice president was not keen on the idea of the Twenty-fifth Amendment, fearing more uprisings from antifa.

Members of Congress did not want to believe that the violence was caused by antifa because they believed that they really did not exist and that it was only an ideology and nothing else. They desperately wanted to believe it was supporters of the president, even though at many of the past protests, the supporters were never violent. The Congress shows feigned concern for the takeover of the Capitol after many months of silence from them during the many months cities were burning down, people were being beaten and killed, as well as police officers being injured and killed. Police stations burned down, parts of a city occupied by thugs, and no one in Congress batted an eye but now because the protesters were possibly supporters of the president, it was an issue.

Then on TV, they broke in with a special report from the White House. Congress, led by a vindictive old female, presses for an impeachment of the president for his incitement to incursion of the Capitol. But there is no evidence for this charge as well as in the speech the president gave to his crowd. The Democrats wanted a swift and unjust impeachment so as to not allow the president to run for office again. So they pushed the attempt to start the sham impeachment without giving the president any due process or to present any evidence.

We were always preached to that the Constitution is our standard of governance, but the Democrats run roughshod over it all the time. This move by Congress made the violent members of antifa and BLM as well as their supporters in the Congress very happy. The president was stepping down from his position as the president of the United States before the impeachment because as a private citizen, he could not be impeached, thus leaving the door open for a second run for the office. The house leader was beside herself for not moving quicker with a vote on impeachment.

Everyone was glued to the TV, and Washington DC came to a halt. The president was in the Oval Office at his desk, and he said, "My fellow Americans, it is with a heavy heart that I am resigning from the presidency effective twelve noon tomorrow. The Democrats in the House want to impeach me to keep me from running for office again, so by resigning, I will still be able to as they cannot impeach a private citizen. This is due to the unforeseen actions of a terror group known as antifa and BLM creating chaos and death at the Capitol. A closer look at who was doing most of the damage shows a large group of white supremacists as well as antifa. The fake news wants us to believe that the culprits in this were my supporters. They were not.

"Information has also surfaced that the riots were preplanned well before my speech, and this will be investigated. Most of the federal and local law enforcement had information that domestic terror groups were coming to DC, but that information fell on deaf ears. Let me ask you, after all my rallies I have had, and there were many of them, have you ever seen any of my supporters wearing helmets, carrying shields, attacking law enforcement? The answer is *no*. The people that did these terrible deeds were not my supporters, only terrorists that hate the country, and please remember that. The only graffiti discovered on the interior walls of the Capitol was 'rock and roll lives.' The feds knew that antifa was big with rock and roll and their clubs.

"We have accomplished many great things for our country, from rebuilding the military, to the VA, large tax cuts, Operation Warp Speed, cutting regulations, high stock market, bringing peace to the Middle East, and so much more. But I am still convinced that we were wronged, but now we must move on for the sake of the country. The vice president has been sworn in as president and commander in chief. I want to thank my administration and staff for all they have done for the American people, which was my first priority. Maybe the truth will come out one day and hopefully soon. Antifa must be destroyed, or we will not have a country anymore. I will go back to my life as a civilian and be ever grateful for the opportunity to make America great again. God bless you, God bless our troops, and God bless America."

The president then got up from the desk and shook the hands of his staff, and as one of his staff, a young man, reached out to shake the president's hand, a small tattoo was noticed on the top of his hand; it was the insignia of antifa. The president then walked calmly to his desk and pressed the panic button under the desk. This immediately alerted the Secret Service right outside his office. Several agents rushed in as the president told them to secure this guy, meaning the young man. Underneath this guy's dress shirt was a T-shirt that said, "rock and roll rules." The staffer turned out to be a mole for antifa. One of the agents is overheard saying that he could not believe this all started at a rock-and-roll club in Florida years earlier. How the FBI missed this during their vetting was unbelievable. The president left the White House with his security detail and got on *Marine One* to the airport then onto *Air Force One* for the flight back to Florida. The vice president then went on TV to tell the American public and our adversaries that all was well and under control then went off the air.

Now that the president was gone, a person came forward, and not just any person. This person was the owner of the rock-and-roll club named The Hurt. He now has information about how the club got its name and its background and it relates to the start of antifa from the early '80s. South Florida was a new breeding ground for homegrown terror groups unbeknown to many, especially law enforcement. There was a lot of hatred of the law and law enforcement. Rumors were spreading for many years about an organization that was against fascism and our government. But no one had any proof of any wrongdoing; neither did anyone ever come forward with personal information about anyone fitting that description. Many thought this would fade away like the Weather Underground did in the '60s.

But this suspicious group had one thing in common, and it was rock and roll. They felt that rock music was loud and anti-government, which was what they believed in. This group started out small with mini attacks across Florida, just enough to keep people on their toes without killing anyone. Many of their members, who were increasing monthly, were pedophiles, which was very odd. They felt that if law enforcement was busy with them, they could hide in plain sight. As the years progressed, several of the pedophiles slipped into legitimate businesses such as rock-and-roll clubs, as that music was loud and the people were wild. In the early '70s, a club was found to be a good fit for the upcoming terror group and pedophiles. It was owned by an elderly gentleman who was looking to get out of the business.

He owned the club that was named The Hurt. What the group liked was that it had a very deep basement for storage of any kind. No one back then knew how much the anti-government group would get and how violent it would become. Who knew that one of the past owners was a pedophile murderer of children and had their bodies buried in the basement? The FBI was amazed that the antifa roots went far back in time and that they were involved with child lovers.

Now that the president was out of office, he was still involved with the party and the media still hounded him. He had always disavowed antifa and BLM and had them deemed a terror organization. He then heard that the FBI was discovering on a daily basis that it was not him that caused the lunatics to riot, but many that were members of antifa and white nationalists. The riot appeared to be preplanned days in advance. Then one psychotic member of Congress made a comment that many of the National Guard on duty at the Capitol were white men that could be involved in a plot for an inside attack on the new president. Thus, the FBI decided along with the Secret Service to vet all members of the guard.

The feds even had intel that there might be some terror members dressed as National Guard and get into the Capitol. Many of the entertainers that were scheduled to perform had backed out because of possible trouble, the parade was cancelled, and now a virtual parade would take place. On the day the new president was inaugurated, there was no trouble; a few protesters showed up but were peaceful. The new president stood before a few and gave his "I hate America" speech. He denounced the white nationalists but not antifa or Black Lives Matter groups because they have his ear in the White House.

After all the fanfare, the new president signed numerous executive orders putting over 50,000 people out of work by shutting down an oil pipeline and the southern border wall, then rejoining the Paris Climate Accord, and getting back into the Iran nuclear deal even as they shouted, "death to America." This guy was a threat to America as he was definitely not an America-first president; he was putting the other countries before this country, and his extreme radical co-conspirators that worked for him would destroy the country. The president even gave an office to BLM in the White House. The Republicans in Congress were beside themselves after what this new president did on his first day.

Several of the new members of Congress could not see how this president who actually lost the election and won by massive fraud could be in office and take this country down the wrong path. In a secret meeting, these Republicans were hatching a plan to take out this president, and they would use their special military experience to do it. In just a short time, antifa got word of this plot and contacted some of these Republicans to help in their endeavor. It became known that one of the new Republicans' parents, now deceased, went to a club in South Florida in the '80s when the craziness with antifa apparently was born and the parents were eventually killed in the fire that destroyed the club.

These Congress people did not want to work with these animals. These Congress people would like to destroy antifa as they were violent and anti-American. The congressmen had a hook in the White House, a rogue Secret Service agent who worked with the previous president and his allegiance was not to the new president. But it was going to be tricky getting this agent to violate his oath; these guys were very serious people and believed in democracy, but he would assist when asked. This small group of congressmen was planning a coup, and they knew that if caught, they would be imprisoned or killed.

But they were true patriots and could not just sit on their hands while the country was turned into a social nightmare. They had a date in mind, and it was soon; probably within a month, the plan would be enacted. They knew that the longer they waited, the more the country went down the toilet. The plan would be a quick armed entry into the front gate, taking out the agents and their dogs. Guns with silencers would be used as well as knives, then a quick run up to the Oval Office, where the president would be reviewing his horrible policies with an advisor. Then a hack into the security system of the White House would prevent anyone from alerting the police and any other agent.

Meanwhile, a car would be brought up to the residence for the getaway. Quick entry into the Oval Office and then kill any advisors before grabbing the president. He would then be taken to the waiting car and removed from the property, probably under heavy gunfire. The attack team would have snipers on some of the rooftops nearby to take out the snipers on top of the White House. The president would then be taken to a boat on the Potomac to a safe house at an unknown location. While there, he would be interrogated as to why he wants to destroy the country and stop all the good the previous president had accomplished. Why kowtow to the far-left lunatics? So this was the plan that was hatched by these rogue congressmen.

But it looked like some might be getting cold feet as they were hesitant to speak about their endeavor. But after a few days, they came around and were all in now. The team decided on a day that was a holiday, and most of the staff would be out of town and many of the agents gone also. It was midwinter and snowing; the trees and grounds were covered in snow, a very pretty sight with the White House and Capitol lit up. The agents working outside were wearing thick coats that covered their weapons, and their dogs were in their kennels. The attack team were all in place at a local bar, sitting in a dark corner and finalizing their horrific plan to kidnap the president of the United States.

They knew their actions would have a worldwide effect and not a good one, but at this point, they did not really care. They were totally disgusted with this fake president who was out to destroy the country, and they would do anything to save it. So they said a prayer and suited up. They got into their car, checked all their weapons and ammo as well as body armor. The team of four rolled up to the north side of the guard site. They saw two agents sitting inside. Two of the team snuck up on the security office and fired into it, killing the agents. They then climbed the fence and entered the security office and lowered the tire deflaters.

Then their hired snipers took out the agents on top of the White House and several more that came running from the quarters along with their dogs. Then the security system was shut down by a team member. They then made their way to the Oval Office, where the president was sitting and alone, luckily. The team members walked up and opened the Oval Office doors and immediately grabbed the president and put a gag over his mouth. They quickly carried him to the waiting car and were quick to get away and to their waiting boat. The team had hired a couple of losers to help and pilot the boat. Meanwhile as they reached the boat, the call went out of the breach and attack at the White House.

Numerous law enforcement personnel and helicopters responded within minutes. The entire area was shut down, airports notified as well as seaports. The stock markets were notified to halt trading and the armed forces put on alert in case our foes decided to do something stupid.

The vice president was immediately taken to a safe area and under guard. The Speaker of the House was also notified along with the Senate leader. Unfortunately, there was no description of the getaway car since the security system also shut down the cameras. The boat now had the rogue congressmen, the president, and the two morons that had the boat. They quickly took off and totally away from downtown DC.

The congressmen didn't want to hurt the president, just get him to reverse course on his policies for the country. Under the cover of darkness, the boat pulled up to a dock, and they got out to a parked car. The two guys of the boat left and were never heard from again, but the congressman knew where they lived. The congressmen and the president get into the car and drive to a nondescript house in downtown Maryland. They get into the house, where they make the president very comfortable and actually apologize to him for what they have done. They tell the president why they did what they did and feel bad about the lives of the agents lost.

They get the president a cup of coffee and some medication he takes on a daily basis. The president tells the congressmen that understands why they did this but that they have to know this means life in prison or death for them. He tells them, "You could have just made an appointment to see me to discuss the issues." One congressman tells the president that although this was a very extreme kidnapping, it was the only way. He continues by asking the president why he did not come out against the BLM group or antifa. They were destroying the country in many ways, but no one on the Dems' side seemed to care, only attacking Republicans and conservatives. The president tells these congressmen, "The previous admin was heading in the wrong direction, and we had to come in to correct things before they got out of control." He continued, "Antifa is just an ideology that is misguided, and we have learned why they are destructive."

One of the congressmen continued to interrogate the president but was not getting any good answers, so he threatened harm to the president if he was not more forthcoming. One of the congressmen told the president, "The previous president knew that antifa was a group of domestic terrorists and deemed them so, so why don't you?"

Then the FBI got a phone call from an unknown man with an accent. He told them about their involvement in the kidnapping of the president but wanted to make a deal if they turned themselves in. The FBI told him that the FBI does not negotiate with terrorists. The suspect then told the FBI that the president would never be seen or heard from again. He continued, "I and my friend will never be found unless we can make a deal for jail time." The FBI told the suspect that they would have to get with their boss, the FBI director, to discuss this further. The suspect told the FBI, "Do not take long because we will then forever disappear." The FBI told the suspect to call back later in the day for a decision.

Approximately six hours later, the suspect called the FBI back and was told that they would make a deal to get the president back. Approximately six hours later, the suspect called the FBI and said that they would turn themselves in, but they wanted an attorney but could not afford one. The FBI told him that one would be appointed free of charge. Then the FBI gave a remote location for them to surrender. They were told to come unarmed and with no one else. The suspect agreed and got the surrender location. The FBI picked a location away from the population and spying eyes. The surrender was to be in approximately four hours. The suspect told the FBI what type of car they would be in and what they were wearing.

The FBI alerted their SWAT team and set up in the surrender location. After the FBI was in place, four hours passed, then five hours, then six hours. But then a large dust cloud from the roadway appeared, and it was the two suspects running late. The FBI SWAT team had their rifles on their targets in case they did something threatening. The suspects' vehicle got closer and then came to a stop. None of the suspects got out but just sat in the car. The FBI saw them looking around so as to check out the area. Then the passenger door opened slowly, and the FBI saw a leg come from the front passenger side.

Then the suspect bolted from the car, carrying a gun, running away from the FBI. Then a shot was heard, and the suspect fell dead to the ground. A SWAT member felled the fleeing armed suspect as the driver was yelling, "Don't shoot, don't shoot!" The FBI ordered him from the car, to get out slowly with hands in the air. The SWAT team had this guy right in their sights. The suspect complied and lay on the ground as the FBI moved in to handcuff him. He was in shock and had pleaded with his friend to just give up and not run. But he chose a different way to go. The SWAT team walks over to the dead suspect and turns him over to see writing on his shirt, saying "ANTIFA LIVES." The crime scene was secured, and the FBI evidence recovery team responds along with the FBI Internal Affairs unit. The Medical Examiner also responded for the removal of the body for autopsy. The surviving suspect was taken in by the FBI for interrogation.

Once at the FBI office, they immediately took the suspect into an interview room and read him his rights. "You have the right to remain silent. Anything you say can and will be used against you in a court of law. You have the right to an attorney. If you cannot afford an attorney, one will be appointed to you at no charge. Do you understand your rights?" The suspect stated he understood and wanted a lawyer before he spoke. The FBI stepped out and waited for the attorney. Within hours, the attorney arrived and went in to speak with his client. After approximately one hour, the attorney left the room and met with the FBI agents, telling them, "He is ready to hear the deal you promised and then he will make a statement."

The FBI got with attorneys with the DOJ to discuss what type of deal they could offer to get the president back safely. They had questions like "Do we give full immunity, partial immunity, minimal jail time, or let him go without any charges?" The FBI said, "Until we hear what he has to say, we cannot offer any deal and his information has to be checked to see if it is substantiated." They then met with the vice president.

The DOJ and FBI briefed the VP, and she was not happy with any of the possible deals because she did not like making deals with terrorists. After this meeting, the FB and DOJ met with the suspect and gave him the possible decisions that were discussed.

The suspect told the feds that anything less than a walk wouldn't do, and the president would be dead. Against their better judgment, they agreed to no jail time. The suspect then started to spell out the congressmen's plans after capture, and the plans were very intricate. The suspect started by saying that the congressmen really don't want to hurt the president. They needed this drastic measure to get the attention of the rest of Congress and the White House. He continued, stating that the congressmen were a Trojan horse and that they were members of antifa who felt that the president's administration was hurting their cause but not to an extreme.

The congressmen didn't want the country burned down like the very extreme antifa members but to repair some of the hurtful executive orders that were in play. The congressmen had family members that were killed in the rock-and-roll club fatal fire in South Florida and they were against that type of violence. The FBI agent asked, "So where are they?" The suspects said that the president was to be held in an abandoned building in Maryland. At that building, they had stockpiled a massive amount of ammo and explosives to be used if necessary. The suspect was not sure of the address but could draw a map from memory as he had been there before.

The map was pretty detailed and given to the FBI agents, who then called in some undercover agents to go by the building on a recon mission. The undercover agents obtained an old-model van and drove by the abandoned building. The got the address and returned to the office. Upon their arrival, they told the other agents that there was a small light on in one of the upper floors and a small four-door vehicle out back. This information was given to the FBI SWAT team as they prepared for the assault. A team of fifteen SWAT team members geared up and planned their assault.

Upon their approach, also out with them were paramedics and special agents. The SWAT team approached from their van very slowly, wearing all black and carrying automatic weapons. As they approached the front door, they found it to be locked. They used plastic explosives on the gate lock and blew it off. They very quickly moved into the building and up the stairs and made a dynamic entry into the room where the president was presumably in. But to their surprise, it was empty. Then they heard footsteps on the floor above, so they quickly responded there.

At the same time, the FBI helicopter was overhead, shining its spotlight on the roof. As the FBI got closer to the suspects, they started taking on gunfire. The suspects then got onto the roof, with nowhere else to run. The helicopter's spotlight was on them, but they then started to shoot at the helicopter. Then they got into an all-out gun battle with the FBI, and after several minutes, it was all quiet. No agents were injured. As they cautiously approached a hidden corner of the rooftop, they saw the president lying dead from several bullet wounds.

Two of the suspect congressmen were also dead. At this point, it was not clear who killed the president, the suspects or the SWAT team. It would take the investigation to determine as the SWAT team surrounded the dead president as their last act of protection until his body is removed.

The vice president was immediately notified of the death of the president, which sends the country into a tailspin. Other countries around the globe take notice as the United States military is put on notice as NORAD was keeping an eye on those countries who would do us harm, like China, North Korea, and Russia. Antifa members from around the globe went into hiding, fearful of the governments coming after them and eliminating them. They had just taken down the biggest prize in the world, the president of the United States, and many leaders around the world were fine with it.

Many of the rock-and-roll clubs throughout the country that were operated by antifa members or funded by them folded up and disappeared into the night. NORAD saw no military movements from any other country, but they kept their guard up anyway. The VP shut down trading on the stock exchange and both houses of Congress were brought in to deal with the emergency. The chief justice of the Supreme Court was brought to the White House to swear in the VP as president, and the country went wild and not in a good way. The new president was a very radical person and had very radical ideas and policies for the country.

She was not pro-America, and it was an America-last ideology. She had no problem with groups like antifa and BLM as she felt they were just frustrated with the way the country was going and that they needed to be brought around. Other groups like the Proud Boys and the white supremacists were her enemies, and she would crush them but not the other two radical groups. As the Congress was preparing for the presidential funeral, chatter was picked up by the FBI about some type of trouble brewing in downtown DC. This was relayed to the Secret Service and to the president.

The Secret Service and the Capitol police requested that a high fence be in place during the funeral as a precaution. The park police got the fencing and started to have it put up. The FBI started their criminal investigation into the kidnapping of the president and the deaths of the federal agents. The ballistics unit of the FBI lab ran tests on all the guns that the SWAT team used as well as the bad guys' guns to see who killed the president. This would take time, but it was a priority for the FBI. The investigation took the FBI to the White House, a diner, the boat and the Maryland warehouse.

After a few days, the ballistics report came in and it was devastating; the bullet that killed the president came from the SWAT leader. The FBI now had to meet with that person to break the news to him. The FBI went to the SWAT leader's home and went in to speak with him. The FBI agent said, "I'm sorry to have to tell you this, but it was your bullet that killed the president." The SWAT leader then sat in his chair with his head in his hands and saying, "Oh my god. Now what?" he asked. The FBI told him he had to come to their office for a statement, but they knew, in the fog of war, bad things happen that are not criminal.

The FBI told him to come into their office the following day for the statement. He said that he would be there. Back in South Florida, there was a secret party given by antifa, and they invited members of BLM. They wanted the BLM group to take the pressure off their organization while they regrouped. The FBI wanted to know how deep this insurrection went since this started in the White House. Now BLM felt empowered to do something on a big scale. They gathered at a meeting hall to discuss their attack on the populace. They had been known to pick fights with anyone, young and old.

They flew their stupid flag above the American flag, burned the flag, broke out store windows, burned buildings, attacked the police and firefighters. They harassed and threatened political leaders and presidents, but the White House stayed quiet. Why? Because they were a good voting bloc for the Democrats. The DOJ and FBI were not fond of this group and knew how dangerous they can be. But they faced a White House that coddled the BLM group. The feds got their marching orders from the new president on how to deal with BLM. This did not sit well with the heads of the two departments.

They would not obey the order from the president as they felt it was an unlawful order, and they instructed their underlings to also ignore the presidential order. The BLM members belonged in jail or dead, said one official from the agency. This problem was brought to Congress as they have a say in it. The Congress heard from the department heads of the FBI and DOJ about what the president had ordered. After days of congressional meetings, they sided with the department heads. This decision did not sit well with the president, so she fired both department heads.

The president had no time to battle with Congress over this incident as she was working on the presidential funeral. As this was going on, the investigation into how the president was shot and killed went on. The FBI agent was being interviewed. As the FBI got their information, they sent it to the DOJ attorneys. The DOJ reviewed the case notes and decided that in the fog of war, bad things happen, and the FBI agent would not be charged with anything, but the he would be branded the killer of the president.

The FBI agent was very relieved but saddened that it was his bullet that killed the president. He then went back to his unit and back to work. Meanwhile, the president's funeral was planned out along with the Secret Service. The president would lie in the Capitol Rotunda for several days, then be taken to Arlington Cemetery for burial along with music, a military flyover and taps. Many dignitaries would be in attendance as well as several world leaders; this would be a security nightmare. Extra police and federal officers from around the country would be brought in to help secure the funeral.

The Capitol police along with the Secret Service would be the inner security ring, and everyone else would be the outer ring. DC would be shut down two days in advance for the arrivals of the world leaders as this would be a major inconvenience to those who live nearby, but they were used to it. The NSA contacted the FBI and Secret Service that they were getting chatter about the funeral event but nothing threatening yet. The feds were on alert for anything that might be out of the ordinary. The air space around DC had also been restricted for a twenty-mile radius. Snipers had been stationed on many of the rooftops around the Capitol and White House.

The feds were expecting large numbers of people that wanted to see the funeral and all the world leaders arriving. But they were kept out from the area with large metal fencing for security concerns. Secretly, members of Congress were planning an extermination squad to once and for all rid the earth of antifa and BLM which only tore down any country they were in. The Congress would solicit the assistance of Israel's secret police and military along with the US military and the intelligence communities. This would be a large undertaking and something that was probably illegal, but this drastic measure had to be done.

Americans and others around the globe could not live in fear any longer. While this plan was in progress, the president's funeral started under very heavy security. The funeral went off without any problems and very few incidents of trouble, which were quelled very quickly. All the dignitaries left the country without incident, thanks to the Secret Service and many others. After the funeral, many bystanders remained behind as if they had nowhere else to go, but by nightfall, they were gone.

Back at the secret meeting called Operation Clean Sweep, phone calls were going back and forth between Israel and the United States, and those involved would keep the president out of the loop for her own protection. Many secret warrants would have to be obtained from the DOJ and FISA, many phone calls made to other countries that might be involved. The goal of this operation was to eliminate the terror groups like they did to ISIS. No courts, prison just a mass grave for them. They really don't have an exact count of how many members each group has, but one thing they know is that antifa is very involved in rock-and-roll clubs all over the place, so they will be the main targets of the operation.

Every state would be impacted by this operation and would involve hundreds of specialized law enforcement. The Department of Defense (DOD) would also be tasked with assisting in the operation utilizing SEALs, Green Berets, Rangers, military police, and many other special operators. The teams would work under the cover of darkness and swiftly. This secret meeting was so secret that if information of it leaked, the leaker would face federal charges and mandatory prison time. Many of the warrants had to come from the FISA courts because of their nature and would not be an easy task.

But after the federal attorneys put the many warrants together, they had to get the approval from the secret FISA court. Even after all the secrecy, their plan leaked out, but by whom? The plan was to seek out and kidnap the antifa members and take them to a dark site outside the country and eliminate them. The operation would entail the special operators to visit any of the rock-and-roll clubs managed by antifa or where the members gathered, shut them down, and grab them all. This would be done wherever they existed, either their workplace, home, or their headquarters.

The goal was to break up and eliminate the terror group and to bring peace to those communities that were being terrorized, like the Pacific Northwest. But now the ACLU was making a lot of noise after seeing and hearing the leak of information. They filed a complaint with the DOJ to halt any more subpoenas and to investigate whoever put this operation together and, if need be, to send those involved to prison. So like any good politician would, the operational plan was scrapped by those involved, and all evidence of the plan destroyed. Now the country was back to the original problem of how to deal with the antifa terror group.

They were now hoping that some vigilante group like the Proud Boys or some other pro-America group would take action. The FBI had a meeting with the president to discuss the rise of domestic terrorism in the country, speaking about BLM, antifa, Proud Boys, White supremacists, and a few others. But oddly enough, the president did not want to talk about the Black Lives Matter group as she and her staff felt they were not the problem in the country. So one of the FBI agents said, "I guess talk about killing cops and defunding the police is OK with you, Madam President?" The president did not like what she heard and asked the agent to leave, which he gladly did.

He then immediately made a call to his friend outside the agency who was a member of the Proud Boys. The agent was overheard talking about eliminating some group but unsure what group. Now that the operational plan was dissolved, the pressure was put on the state governors to take police action. The main states were Washington, Oregon, and Washington DC. But these states were run by Democrats who could not care less about antifa burning down the cities, looting, and killing cops.

The best the vigilantes could do was to go to South Florida each year on the anniversary of the rock-and-roll club disaster, when hundreds of antifa gathered to remember their friends. There was chatter heard from possible Proud Boys talking about forming their own vigilante squad and going after the antifa thugs. But it went on without any response from the FBI. They blew it off as just talk without any plan of action. The Proud Boys movement had grown exponentially and was believed to be heavily armed at all times. They did not care much about dying as long as they could take out as many of the antifa and BLM members they could across the country.

So later in the month, the antifa members gathered at the spot of the old rock-and-roll club in South Florida. The Proud Boys decided that this was their opportunity to get the job done as there would be probably several hundred antifa and BLM members there. So the Proud Boys made their calls to arms and brought together their minions and responded to the South Florida gathering. It was now a Friday night and dark out. The only lights were two streetlights and some headlights from parked cars. The local police had the area blocked off for the gathering, for which they had a permit.

Then it was time for the attack. Many of the Proud Boys surrounded the gathering without being noticed as others fanned out in the parking lots. Their plan was to take out their machine guns that fired hundreds of rounds per minute, creating a killing field, and those who ran for cover to their cars were mowed down by the other Proud Boys, hopefully leaving most dead. Then they got the word as members of antifa and BLM stood side by side, praying for their lost friends. Then numerous gunshots seemed to come from everywhere. The gathering started to fall to the ground, most dead, and as others attempted to flee, they were caught in the gunfire by the other Proud Boys in the parking lots.

The few police officers heard the multiple gunshots and ran toward it and also took fire. They were able to return fire, taking out several of the Proud Boys as many of the others fled the area. When the smoke cleared, hundreds from the gathering lay dead or dying. The police called for multiple reinforcements and paramedics. There was so much confusion on the scene most of the Proud Boys escaped. As many other officers arrived and walked through the carnage, numerous weapons were scatted on the ground. Several of the victims were still alive and rushed to the hospital but died on the operating table.

A call went out to mutual aid to help with the massive crime scene. The FBI and ATF were also involved in this mass murder. It was going to take many days of working the crime scene and attempting to identify the victims and the suspects that fled. Word got out pretty quick of the mass shooting, resulting in numerous media outlets showing up. The airport and highway police were notified of the fleeing felons, but there was very limited information on what they looked like and the vehicles they were in.

The Congress heard about the shooting and immediately blamed the former president like they always did. Meanwhile, outside the former president's residence, people were starting to gather, with signs protesting and believing the former president had something to do with the mass murder. His spokesman immediately put out a statement that the former president had nothing to do with the shooting and disavowed the Proud Boys. But that did not dissuade the protesters, but when more law enforcement showed up, they left quietly. Of course, now the lamestream media was telling everyone that the former president was responsible for the mass murder and he should face first-degree murder charges as well as those who pulled the trigger.

The president was not saying those inflammatory words but was probably thinking them. Back in Portland, Seattle, and NYC, police and the FBI are waiting at the airports for any of the Proud Boys returning from South Florida. Dozens were detained as they exited the planes and then were taken into custody for interrogations. Some of these brainless morons still had the bloodstained clothes on from when they did the shooting. They were immediately detained and handcuffed and taken away by the FBI and local PD. When the feds retained the luggage, they found the firearms used in the murders. All the airports mentioned had numerous Proud Boy members in them, and they too were detained.

All in all, several dozen were arrested, and many weapons seized. All that were detained were quickly arraigned in federal court and held without bail. Several foreign airports in France and Germany had their law enforcement stop and detain suspects coming from South Florida. Back at the mass crime scene, some of the victims were being identified, and to the FBI's surprise, several of the victims were congressional aides to some high-powered congressmen. Now the FBIs had to broaden their net to possibly include some members of Congress. The president was briefed on this and ordered her Secret Service to repeat a background check on all the congressional staff.

After those arrested in Europe went to prison, word got out to the terror bosses, and they hatched an escape plan to get their boys back. Late one afternoon while numerous Proud Boys members were in an outdoor recreation field, a large low-flying helicopter flew over the yard as someone in the chopper dropped smoke bombs onto the field. This diverted the attention of the guards as the chopper lowered a rope ladder for the convicts to climb up and escape. Four very quickly made it to the chopper and climbed the ladder into the chopper as they came under gunfire. People in the chopper returned fire as a fifth attempted to get to the ladder, but he was gunned down by a tower guard before he got into the chopper.

The chopper took off quickly with four escapees. No guards were injured during the escape. The escape was big news as all law enforcement were alerted. This escape got all the way to the White House, where the president was briefed. The president's personal security was doubled for his safety. The helicopter made a clean getaway and was later found in a field near a small secret airport. It was believed that the suspects, including the pilot, escaped in a small-engine plane, whereabouts unknown. The FBI was picking up chatter about the escape at the foreign prison and, after talking with their intelligence counterparts, was able to locate an area where the escapees might be holed up.

The FBI offered their help in capturing the suspects, but their help was turned down. The suspects were traced to an old barn house just outside Paris and known to their military. They formulated a plan of attack hoping to catch all involved unharmed, but it was not to be. The military surrounded the barn house and transmitted orders for them to surrender. The suspects yelled back that they would not go back to prison, at which time they opened fire on the military. The heavily armed military returned fire with their cannons from their tanks, obliterating the barn house and everyone in it.

This was very unfortunate as the FBI wanted them alive to interview them. It was obvious the military could not care less if there were any survivors.

Back in the States, the feds were getting ready for the trials, and they had ordered the police to beef up security inside and outside the courthouse. The judges involved as well as the prosecutors were given extra security. Limited access to the courthouse was established, and only those with a security ID were allowed in. The first day of the trial, several bomb threats were called in, delaying the trial. This went on for several days, with many interruptions as each threat had to be taken seriously. The presiding judge had enough of the delays and ordered the trial to be moved onto a local military base where security is always at its highest. This did not sit well with the defense attorneys as it would limit the amount of concerned personnel allowed at the trials.

But then out of the blue, the suspects in the case pleaded guilty to a lesser crime, and they were given lighter sentences. This made the prosecution very suspicious, and they started their investigation into the reason why they pleaded guilty after fighting so hard for a trial.

The federal investigation was turned over to the FBI. This would probably take some time as investigations in DC took forever. Then for some time, you never heard of the Proud Boys as they went deep underground. The antifa mob started to show up at the courthouses and prisons in support of the Proud Boys although they were really enemies. They felt that if they joined forces even with different ideologies, they could make a big statement in the country.

This would be a force to deal with if this was to happen. Two domestic enemies of the country would really keep the law enforcement community very busy. The FBI had been tracking both of the organizations and felt that they could not let these two forces combine into one. The FBI discovered that the marching orders were coming from a guy in Portland and found where he was calling from, so the Portland FBI office and relayed the information to them. The Portland

FBI obtained a search warrant for the target residence and got their SWAT team in on the warrant.

The FBI/SWAT team had their briefing and went out to execute the warrant. They got with the Portland police to cover the nearby streets for traffic as well as to transport suspects, if any. SWAT moved in very quietly then broke down the front door then threw in several flash-bangs to disorient anyone in the home. There was screaming and yelling as the SWAT team moved through the house. They found a guy on his computer, wearing headphones. This guy looked surprised as he never heard any of the SWAT team enter. They handcuffed the suspect and brought him out of the home as several other FBI agents conducted a search.

They mainly wanted the computers and thumb drives, which they took. But what they did not realize was that the flash-bangs used had caused a fire, and it was spreading very fast. They quickly got out, taking anything they could carry. The fire department was called but by the time they arrived, the fire had substantially spread, destroying the home. The suspect sat in a patrol car as he watched his home burn down. He then yelled out, "My dog, my dog!" But no one saw or heard a dog, and they thought maybe it ran out.

After the fire was finally extinguished and a walkthrough was completed by the fire department, they discovered the suspect's dog dead in a back room. This information was relayed to the FBI and Portland police, who in turn broke the news to the suspect. They told the suspect that his dog was found and that it did not survive the fire. The suspect looked at the FBI in disbelief for several seconds then started to cry and yelled out, "You killed my dog, you killed my dog, you fucking assholes! I'm not talking to you, and I want a fucking lawyer, now." The FBI stopped all questioning until a lawyer was obtained. The FBI really felt that they had the big fish that had all the pertinent information on his violent group and the Proud Boys.

They really wanted to talk with him and his lawyer and were willing to make a good deal with no jail time if he cooperated. Then while the suspect was alone in a room, waiting for his lawyer, he was able to get a pill from his pants pocket and quickly ingest it. Within minutes, the suspect lay dead on the floor, foaming from the mouth. He had taken a cyanide tablet, making him a martyr for the cause. When the FBI came back to the room and discovered their suspect dead, they immediately called for medical, but it was too late. Now they had a lot of explaining to do on how they missed that pill in his pocket. At least the feds had the computers and thumb drives to continue the investigation.

Secretly they could not care less that this guy was dead. As the FBI investigation moved forward, they discovered emails showing that the attacks were preplanned and not spontaneous as they thought earlier. The DOJ had their attorneys working overtime on warrants and subpoenas to be served quickly before the members truly disappeared and evidence was destroyed. The FBI, ATF, US Marshals, and many local police department SWAT teams would serve the high-risk warrants. The national and local media were also invited to witness the operations and any arrests.

The family of the suspect that committed suicide filed a formal complaint against the agents and the FBI for wrongful death in the suicide of their son, stating that if the FBI did their job properly and searched their son properly, they would have found the pill and their son would still be alive. The family knew it was a long shot suing the federal government and attorney's fees can be substantive. But time would tell. Then back on the west coast of the country, antifa was active again and were having a large gathering, which put the city on lockdown again. Most were happy to see the Proud Boys go down as they did, and now they could move forward in their destructive actions again. Many of the businesses were boarded up and the owners got out for their safety as their police department again did nothing to stop the scourge. The group marched down the main avenue, smashing windows that were not boarded up, setting fires and burning the American flag, yelling "death to America!" These scumbags needed to be eliminated from the earth, but the Democrats had different ideas. They wanted them in their party of hate and in the administration. They also wanted their votes, which is what it always was about.

CHAPTER 14

Then a large group of lawmen had just had enough of the antics of antifa and their attacks on them and their families. As lawmen were pushing back a massive group of haters, they opened fire on them. Massive amounts of bullets were fired in rapid succession. Dozens of antifa members fell dead to the ground, and those were still moving were shot again and killed. It was like a John Wick movie. As the shooting was happening, numerous other antifa members fled for their stinking lives. Some were walking wounded and wound up in the hospital emergency rooms from gunshots. After the shooting, the officers involved turned themselves in to internal affairs.

They all told the same story that they were in fear for their lives, so they defended themselves. The internal affairs detectives then closed the cases as did the prosecutors; as you can imagine, this did not sit well with the terror group, who now threatened revenge. Antifa was looking for an all-out war against the establishment, and their numbers were growing. A special prosecutor was brought in to prosecute this case, and this guy was a true hard ass. He did not believe in someone defending themselves with flimsy evidence to back it up. He filed a motion to throw out that claim with the judge, and after the judge reviewed it, that motion was upheld, meaning there was no self-defense claim.

Now the accused had to come up with a more plausible explanation to their shooting, which they did not have. So now their attorneys went to the special prosecutor, and they were looking for a deal instead of a trial. The prosecutor told the defense attorney to wait a few days while he looked further into the case. After a few days, all the attorneys had a meeting and came up with a plea deal. All defendants would serve a maximum of twenty-five years without parole, in lieu of the death penalty. This plea somewhat calmed the community down, but the leaders of the terror group were not pleased and vowed revenge.

The terror group still wanted revenge on the cops. So the police command got some of the leaders of the group into a meeting to discuss their threats towards law enforcement in an attempt to calm the waters. These police commanders were afraid of the terror group and pretty much gave into their demands. They demanded taking off the street any cop degrading the movement, partially defunding the police, putting a member of the group on the police civilian board. And after deliberating, the police command agreed to the crazy demands. This enraged so many of the police in that department that half put in their papers to retire and resign.

The antifa and BLM crowd were loving it and happy to see many in the department leave. Then came a series of bombing attacks within the city. They were small bombings but enough to damage property and kill people. One of the bombings killed the bomb maker and gave the cops a lot of evidence to use to find others that might be involved. The FBI and ATF joined in the investigation. Luckily, the only person killed so far was a bomb maker. But they were not sure if there were any other bombs planted somewhere out there. The terror leaders felt the only thing the government knew was force and threats tied into terror.

The FBI had warned several of the federal agencies that there were threats made toward the establishments and those who worked in the buildings. The House Speaker in DC and the local police were instructed to erect a large metal fence encompassing the entire building, and it was to be manned by the local police and federal police. The president offered the National Guard, but it was denied by the police chief and speaker. Then one afternoon, there were large crowds starting to form outside some of the federal buildings. This frightened the speaker as she now called for the National Guard from the military generals.

The president was on board and the military authorized the National Guard by the thousands, approximately 25,000, and they were to be fully armed and loaded. It was ironic that the Democrats in Congress now liked the police and walls. What a bunch of hypocrites. As many of the guard started to arrive, the crowds got bigger and bigger, some carrying their antifa and BLM flags along with the American flag upside down. Hundreds of local law enforcement were also on the grounds. There was no way anyone was getting over the fencing and into the buildings, and if they did, they would be shot dead.

As night came in, several extremely loud bangs could be heard in the distance along with large flashes of light. Then reports came in that several bombs were set off near less-fortified buildings. The Secret Service was notified, and they told the president. The Secret Service restricted the president's movement until they got an all clear from the outside law enforcement. Word was relayed to the White House that there were many casualties to law enforcement and civilians and that the threat was still out there. This president was always spouting unity, so where was the unity? Damage reports were coming in, and they were not good.

There was damage to the IRS building and Washington Monument. People were trapped and dying as the emergency services units were attempting to make rescues, but it was going slowly because of the danger of the buildings collapsing. Extra security was placed around the Whitehouse and capitol buildings. The FBI then gets some chatter from ANTIFA about the violent activity. The FBI also got an anonymous call stating, "You were warned that it was not over, and we will get justice for our members killed in South Florida and we will not stop and there is nothing you can do." In an extreme move, the White House ordered all airports and seaports halt operation until there was a comprehensive search and rescreening of everyone in and around those facilities.

Also ordered was the halting of vehicle traffic leaving DC to search the vehicles; of course, this was a violation of the Constitution. The FBI also did a second background screening of their people and all the other federal law enforcement as no one was immune. All civilian and military helicopters were up and checking every square inch of the ground for anyone that might be hiding. The president was moved into the secure war room where she could monitor the operations and speak with everyone involved. She was getting updates every half hour, and when she had enough information, she would speak to the country.

As time went on, there were no more bombings. So the president went on TV in a special report. She told the country that her extreme measures were put in place because of the violent nature and threats to the country by antifa. She said, "They will not last long, and as soon as we get all clear from the airports and seaports, all will go back to normal, but we have to remain vigilant, and if you see something suspicious, say something and do not hesitate to call 911 or the FBI hotline." As all this was going on, the US Senate started their congressional investigation.

Law enforcement witnesses and leaders from congress were to be called as witnesses as well as reformed members of antifa and BLM. There were a lot of objections from the Republicans about having testimony from any former member of a terror organization, but they were overridden by the Democrats. Extra security was brought in as these hearings were open to the public. The gallery was packed as the witnesses stated their observations and answered the senators' questions. At times, the testimony got very heated between the Republicans and the former terror groups.

At one point, the questions got so pointed that one of the former antifa members threw a bottle of water in the direction of the Republican senator doing the questioning. The senator was not hit, and the person who threw it was removed and arrested by the Capitol police. A Democratic lawmaker then asked for information on who is leading these groups down the violent paths, but they refused to answer, telling the Democrat they would never give out that information, knowing what might happen to them. The questioning went on for several days and ended where it started, with no new information. Congress then passed a sweeping reform bill targeting the antifa and BLM movements.

This bill would make it a federal felony if you engaged in any violence toward the government or the cities where the violence takes place. There would be a mandatory ten-year prison term attached to the crime. There was overwhelming bipartisan support for a change.

Congress was hopeful that the stiff prison term would quell any future violence, but time would tell. A few weeks later, antifa was marching in downtown Portland, and the march went off without any property destruction or physical violence toward anyone, so it seemed like the bill was a success. The White House and Congress were made aware of this revelation and were happy to see and hear it.

Then a few weeks later, a come-together picnic was advertised for past and current members of the two terror groups to meet up for food and drinks to show that there was no place for any more violence and that they could get their message across without the death and destruction. The police department could now get a break from the violence and long work hours and days. At a White House press briefing, the media was brought up to speed on the coming together of the two groups and law enforcement.

But there were still outstanding warrants for many who had yet to be captured. Also, in the previous mentioned bill if there are no flare-ups in the next five years, the terrorist designation would be removed. So five years passed, and the State Department removed the terror label, with the president's approval. But since it was all these years later, a new president was in place who had a different view of the two questionable groups, and at a peace signing of the two groups in the Oval Office, the president shook the hands of several past members and one reporter noticed a tattoo on the presidents right lower arm, it was the antifa symbol. The conspiracy continues.

Lightning Source UK Ltd.
Milton Keynes UK
UKHW011845190521
384027UK00008B/371/J

9 781664 174061